Soonawissakit, the toughest, most jock-oriented, most Establishment establishment in the East, was Dad's old camp, and I hoped he'd appreciate my following in his footsteps—or trying to.

Well, in February, it had seemed like a good idea—especially since Duck had said he'd go if I'd go, and then Annabel got herself a job there as administrative assistant—but on June 30th, as I stood in the Port Authority terminal, surrounded by those lockjawed jocks in their dirty Adidas, I knew it had all been a terrible mistake.

I looked over at Dad, his arm around Mom's shoulder, having a merry old time with a bunch of other parents, and was disgusted with myself. Dad would never have said he'd go to a place he didn't want to go to, just to please another person.

I watched him gracefully excuse himself from the group and head for the men's room.

I silently wished to God I was somewhere else, some*body* else—him, to be exact.

Then I said it out loud to Duck Levine.

MARY RODGERS

Summer Switch

HarperTrophy®
AN IMPRINT OF HarperCollinsPublishers

Harper Trophy® is a registered trademark
of HarperCollins Publishers Inc.

Summer Switch
Copyright © 1982 by Mary Rodgers
All rights reserved. No part of this book may be used or reproduced
in any manner whatsoever without written permission except in the
case of brief quotations embodied in critical articles and reviews.
Printed in the United States of America. For information address
HarperCollins Children's Books, a division of HarperCollins
Publishers, 1350 Avenue of the Americas, New York, NY 10019.

Library of Congress Cataloging-in-Publication Data
Rodgers, Mary.
    Summer switch / Mary Rodgers.
        p.   cm.
    Summary: A boy and his father literally find themselves in each
other's shoes.
    ISBN 0-06-051231-8 (pbk.)
    [1. Fathers and sons—Fiction.]   I. Title.
PZ7.R6155Su   1982   79-2690
[Fic]   AACR2

Revised Harper Trophy edition, 2003

Visit us on the World Wide Web!
www.harperchildrens.com

For Hank & For Tod

One

I suppose, in a funny sort of way, I owe it all to Camp Soonawissakit, because if I hadn't told Dad I wanted to go there in the first place, I wouldn't have been in the Port Authority Bus Terminal on Departure Day (Thursday, June 30th), wishing to God I was somewhere else. Actually, wishing I was some*body* else— my father, to be exact, who was leaving that afternoon for Los Angeles on a business trip.

"I wish I was him," I remarked gloomily to my old friend from school, Duck Levine.

"Who?" said Duck, gazing at a gaggle of Soonawissakiddies, wondering, no doubt, which brawny no-brain I could possibly be envying.

I nodded in the direction of the men's room, where Dad had just disappeared. "My father," I said. "I would give anything to be him right now."

Well, you are not going to believe me, nobody in their right minds could *possibly* believe me, but the next thing I knew, *I* was in the men's room.

In the body of my father.

Standing at a urinal, looking down at . . .

OH WOW!!!

And then— No, wait. Before I go any further, I'd better give you some hard-nosed facts:

I am Benjamin "Ape Face" Andrews, aged twelve. The Ape Face is courtesy of my older sister, Annabel. She named me that when I was five days old, just out of the hospital. She was six and a half (years), and pretty ticked off at my mother for bringing home a brother who looked like a rhesus monkey minus the hair when what she had in mind was a sister who looked like a Barbie doll. I've been trying to make it up to her ever since, but it's only been in the last couple of years she's begun to find me even tolerable. I certainly hope it lasts, because I admire her a lot, I really do.

We live in New York (the we being me, my sister, my mother, my father, and Max the basset)—on 72nd and Central Park West. No, not the Dakota; across the street from the Dakota. Funny, whenever you tell people you live on 72nd and C.P.W., they always ask expectantly, "Oh, the Dakota?" and then when you say, "No, the Majestic, across the street," they say, "Oh." That's all. Just "Oh." Thud. You'd think we lived in a slum dwelling or something, which the Majestic far from is.

I go to the Barden School, where I do pretty well. To be honest about it, except for being only a so-so athlete, I do very well . . . year after year my reports

2

come home with grades in the high 90's and enthusiastic comments about my "extraordinary verbal ability" and about how I am "conscientious," "cooperative," "considerate of others," "a genuine pleasure to teach" . . . everybody thinks I'm perfect, it seems. Well, not quite everybody. There was one teacher, my third-grade homeroom teacher, Miss Moon (who moved the end of that year to Beverly Hills, California). She wrote, "Although Ben has maintained his usual high standard of academic excellence, I must admit to being somewhat disappointed in his performance in other areas. For an exceptionally bright child, he displays a perplexing tendency to 'lay back'—to accept unquestioningly the word of authority, whether it be in the schoolroom or the playground. It is my hope that if Ben is encouraged both at school and at home to become more outspokenly assertive, he may ultimately be able to realize his enormous potential as a leader in the Barden community. At the present time, however, he is entirely too agreeable for his own good."

You should have heard my father. He had a fit. "You just try being *dis*agreeable and see where that gets you!" he said, eyebrows raised.

"Tee-hee," went Annabel. She knew where it got her. Time after time. As a matter of fact, Annabel was probably largely responsible for my being the way I was. Watching her get into trouble provided great incentive for staying out of it. If you're someone like

3

me, anyway. (More about that later.)

Dad went on with his fit. "What kind of crazy teacher is she?" he grumbled to my mother. "If she keeps up, you know what we'll have on our hands? A rebel without a cause!"

"Not bloody likely," snorted Annabel.

Mom laughed and patted my cheek. "I doubt it, Willy. It's rather late in the game for this little leopard to change his spots."

"Spots where?" I said, anxiously checking my shirt for signs of ketchup. What a jerk I was in those days.

"I guess Mr. Clean doesn't know his Kipling," guffawed Annabel. I wanted to poke her one. Instead, I smiled and changed the subject.

"Don't worry, Dad. I'm going right on being agreeable no matter what Miss Moon says."

"At least that makes one of you," said Dad with a smirk in Annabel's direction. Undaunted, she smirked back and then stuck her tongue out at him. She's got guts!

Dad turned to me again. "Tell me something, Ben . . ."

Now what? Nervously, I balanced my right foot on the inside of my left knee.

"Stop standing stork," snapped Dad, "and tell me what you *really* think of this Miss Moon."

From his tone of voice, I knew what I was supposed to think of her. Down went my foot. "Oh," I said with a shrug, "she's all right, I guess."

Do you know, to this day I can't believe I said that. "She's all right, I guess"?? ALL RIGHT?! Miss Moon wasn't all right, Miss Moon was wonderful and I adored her. She was young, and round like her name, round from top to bottom like plump pillows—with a round, rowdy laugh. On the blackboard, even her a's and e's were round, and her brackets had a curve and a lilt I could never imitate in a million years. But the best thing about her was an ability to tell it like it is without hurting your feelings. Example: One day, when I was in the second grade (Miss Moon was assistant to Miss Milanowsky then), I was finishing up another painting of a stegosaurus—my eighth that year. It was turning out like the other seven—ugly. Ugly, runny, and unrecognizable. She came by, looked over my shoulder, and then, instead of making some dumb remark like "This is interesting work; tell me about it," which decoded simply means "What in heaven's name *is* that?" Miss Moon said, after a slight pause, "Okay, buddy, I give up."

"It's my usual," I explained.

Miss Moon looked amused. "You're just going to keep doing it till you get it right, is that it, pal?"

"Nobody lives to be a hundred and forty," I said, ripping the paper off the easel. I was about to crumple it up when she took it away from me, objecting, "Hey, hey, hey, where are you going with that?!"

She rolled it into a crinkly, crackly tube and handed it back. "Here. Take it home to your mom. She'll love it."

"That's what you think," I said rudely.

"Oh?" said Miss Moon, extremely surprised. With good reason. After all, Ben is "cooperative," "considerate of others," "a genuine pleasure to teach." Ben would never be *rude*. (More about that later.)

"Well, what do you think?" she asked, looking at me curiously, with her deep-blue eyes. So for the next twenty minutes, while the other kids were at recess on the roof, this is roughly what I told her:

In the past three years, aside from at least two paintings a week, I had also brought home several collages—one of spaghetti, macaroni, and pinto beans (uncooked, of course), my personal handprint in clay (except, due to a mix-up in school, I got Charley Kopple's and I assume he got mine), a wooden dog bed, a Christmas-tree ornament made out of a light bulb covered with red and silver glitter, homemade cranberry sauce, a Styrofoam necklace, and a pomander ball. With the following results: Some guest or other put a cigarette out on the handprint and when Mattie the cleaning lady put it in the dishwasher, it melted. The dog bed, Max absolutely refused to sleep in. Growled at me—*me*, his favorite!—when I tried to make him. Annabel hung the Christmas-tree ornament at the back of the tree where no one could admire it except the people at the Dakota. The cranberry sauce, my mother put in the back of the fridge and forgot all about until the Sunday after Thanksgiving, when there was no more turkey to eat it with, so she fed it to Max, who'll eat anything. Just to prove my point, Max also ate the Styrofoam necklace and got so sick it cost us a hundred dollars at the vet. And the pomander ball went bad because of a reason almost too embarrassing to go into. (The teacher told us to ask our mothers for an orange and a box of cloves, but I thought she said a box of *clothes*. So Mom, figuring the school was having a charity collection, gave me a bunch of Dad's old shirts and some of my outgrown cords. Of course, when I got to school, I instantly realized my mistake. Unfortunately, Brian Hitzigger, the rat who sat next to me, realized it, too. He also realized how anxious I was not to have the whole rest of the class realize it, and generously offered to sell me some of his cloves for *fifty cents a clove!* To make a long story short, a pomander ball with only eleven cloves in it goes bad just about as quickly as an ordinary untreated orange. Revolting!)

As for the paintings and collages, after being Scotch-taped to the fridge for a little while, they always mysteriously vanished, and when questioned about this, Mom would mumble vaguely about having put them away somewhere. Oh yeah? I'm no dummy . . . two paintings a week, times four and a half weeks in a month, times eight months in a school year, over a period of three years comes to two hundred and sixteen rolls of crinkly, crackly paper. There isn't a somewhere anywhere in our apartment big enough to accommodate all that! Somewhere like the garbage is more like it.

"Oh, *dear*," said Miss Moon when I'd finished. "That's quite a saga!"

"Yes," I agreed, tightening my grip on *Stegosaurus Number Eight*. "And since she's going to put this stupid thing in the garbage anyway, I might as well save her the trouble and do it now."

Again I started to crumple it up, and again Miss Moon came to its rescue.

"Ben," she said, palm outstretched, "don't do that. I'd love to keep it for myself."

Baffled but docile as ever, I gave it to her.

"Why? Is it any good?" I asked hopefully.

Miss Moon laughed. "To be perfectly honest, I suppose I've seen better. But it'll be a nice reminder of the first time you trusted me enough to say what you really felt about something. And considering what a strong, silent type you usually are, I'm very flattered indeed."

That's what I mean by telling it like it is without hurting your feelings. By the end of that recess period, Miss Moon had me thinking, "So what if I can't paint, and nobody at home wants the stuff I make. Sean

Connery is probably lousy at arts and crafts, too!" I loved her for that. And I loved her for saying what she said about me in that third-grade report, because she was the only teacher in the whole darn school who didn't think I was perfect. And she was the only person in the whole *world* who had my real number—zero, a cipher. Or at least that's what she felt I was in danger of becoming if I didn't change.

Oh, Miss Moon, Miss Moon, how could I have done that to you, been so disloyal, told Dad you were "all right, I guess" when you were the only person with enough courage, and enough insight into Benjamin "Ape Face" Andrews to tell it like it was! More about that right now—I've put it off as long as I could:

I, Benjamin "Ape Face" Andrews, only son of Ellen Jean and William Waring Andrews, beloved of all elevator men and little old ladies on the street, star of the Barden School, the boy most likely to be invited for a sleep-over—I, the crowd pleaser, the yea-sayer, the boy with the ready smile on his face . . . was a coward. Yes, sirree, four feet eleven and a half inches of Yellow Jell-O. Would you like to know what was behind that ready smile of mine? *Another* ready smile. Ha-ha! Fooled you, didn't I, you thought I was going to say a snarl or something. Oh no, not me. I'd never snarled in my life, never lost my temper.

I had many friends. Many, many friends. It's easy. As long as you're born with a reasonable dose of looks and smarts, and are careful never to make people mad, everybody likes you, I guess. The hard part is figuring out who *you* like—because you're so grateful to people for liking you, it kind of colors your vision when you try to decide what you really think of them.

Who did I really like? I didn't know. Duck Levine, definitely. Annabel, definitely. And Miss Moon, indefinitely—meaning as long as I lived. Mom, sure. Dad . . .?

Well, of course I liked Dad. Who wouldn't? A neat guy, with looks and smarts enough to burn, but unlike yours truly, forceful and unafraid. And successful— Vice President in Charge of East Coast Production, Galaxy Films. He used to be in advertising, but Galaxy meant more creative work and more money—which he always says we're in danger of running short if not completely out of, despite the fact that Mom contributes her salary from the Museum of Natural History. (She's a cultural anthropologist now. Until two years ago when she went back to Columbia, she was just a housewife, but if she heard me saying "just a housewife" she'd kill me. The way she calculates it, if Dad had to hire replacements for each of her various functions as Mother, Cook, Cleaning Lady, Social and Financial Secretary/Hostess, and Interior Decorator, it would cost him $54,060. Furthermore, since she's still doing all that stuff *and* contributing her salary, she says she's worth practically as much as he is.)

Anyway, absolutely, I liked Dad. The question was,

did Dad like me? Oh, I knew he loved me, the way all parents usually love their kids (even Mr. and Mrs. Hitzigger probably love Brian, although it must be quite an effort); but we didn't seem to connect too well. For instance, every night when he came home, he'd say, "How was school?" and I'd say, "Fine, thanks." Then he'd say, "That's good." End of fascinating conversation. I kept having the feeling that if instead of "Fine, thanks" I'd told him I'd accidentally sliced off the tip of my little finger in the jigsaw and fed it to the guinea pig, he'd have still said "That's good," because he hadn't heard me in the first place.

I had a feeling I bored him. I had a feeling that no matter how hard I tried to please him—me, the great crowd pleaser—he was the one person I was never going to please. But I kept working at it anyway— which explains why I told him I wanted to go to Soonawissakit. Soonawissakit, the toughest, the most jock-oriented, most Establishment establishment in the East, was Dad's old camp, and I hoped he'd appreciate my following in his footsteps—or trying to.

Well, in February, it had seemed like a good idea— especially since Duck had said he'd go if I'd go, and then Annabel got herself a job there as administrative assistant—but on June 30th, as I stood in the Port Authority terminal, surrounded by those lockjawed jocks in their dirty Adidas, I knew it had all been a terrible mistake.

I looked over at Dad, his arm around Mom's shoulder, having a merry old time with a bunch of other parents, and was disgusted with myself. Dad would never have said he'd go to a place he didn't want to go to, just to please another person.

I watched him gracefully excuse himself from the group and head for the men's room.

I silently wished to God I was somewhere else, some*body* else—him, to be exact.

Then I said it out loud to Duck Levine. And it was at this precise moment that I found myself at the urinal. Looking down at—as I've said before, oh, wow!

About half a minute went by.

Then on my right I heard, "Anything wrong, Andrews?"

Reluctantly tearing my eyes away, I looked up and over. The owner of the voice had just been introduced to me (Ape Face) outside: Captain Splasher Wilking, Camp Director.

Hastily, I zipped my summerweight flannel fly. Cautiously, I turned to check my reflection in the mirror just to make sure—but yes, it was Mr. Neat Guy, all right—forceful and unafraid . . . and leaving this afternoon for Los Angeles on a fun business trip while Mr. Nice Guy the Coward smiled through four horrible weeks in Moosehead Village, Maine. Hallelujah!

I winked at my wonderful, forceful face. So long, Yellow Jell-O. Hello, Bill!

"Wrong? No, nothing wrong," I said. Boomed, I mean, in a rich baritone. Enthralled by the sound of myself, I added, "I'm just fine, thanks, sir . . . uh . . . Captain," and finished with an involuntary giggle of delight. The giggle came out this melodious chuckle.

"Still the same old Andrews, huh, Andrews?" said the Captain, joining me in a chuckle of his own.

Together, we had this jolly chuckle while each of us tried to think of what to say next. On his way out the door, the Captain finally came up with something.

"You know what," he said, suddenly lapsing into salty seafarin' talk, "I got me some great expectations for that little tadpole a yours."

At that very moment, the little tadpole himself made a jet-propelled entrance into the men's room, stopping short just in time to avoid a titanic collision with the Captain's belly. After several attempts to dodge around each other (that routine where you step to your right, then you step to your left, but the guy opposite does the same thing, so nobody moves off square one), Ape Face, with an uncharacteristically murderous glint in his eye, dove—get this! dove down on all fours and scrambled through the Captain's bowlegs, surfacing at the sink, where he proceeded to hippety-hop up and down in front of the mirror. Right away, I knew it was Dad.

The Captain stared at him suspiciously. "What's he doin'?"

I was nicely nonchalant. "Just trying to get a full-length view of himself, I guess."

"Well, that shouldn't be too difficult," he said, and with a jovial "Yo heave ho and away we go!" he hoisted my flabbergasted father high in the air for a better look.

"How's that, little feller?" he asked.

Two

"Put me down," I squeaked, pummeling Wilking on the back with my puny fists. "Put me down—NOW!"

An indignant scowl replaced the grin on his venerable puss and he abruptly lowered me to the tile floor with a tooth-jolting thump.

"Just who do you think you're talking to, mate? Another outburst like that and I'll beat your butt till it's black and blue!" growled Wilking, exiting in high dudgeon.

"Why good heavens, Ben, what happened to your manners?" remonstrated my . . . father? . . . son? . . . *self?* Who? for Pete's sake!

As a kind of test, I fixed him with a beady stare and said, "Just you wait, Daddy-O, you'll get yours!"

Briefly, the eyes met mine, then fell away. Significant, but not one-hundred-percent conclusive. Then the sole of a Gucci-shod foot inched slowly up the other leg, coming to rest on the inner thigh. Ape Face! Indisputably Ape Face—standing stork. All righty, at least that much had been established. But how this grotesque ectoplasmic transmigration could possibly have happened in the first place was completely beyond me.

Mentally, I ran through the events directly preceding the switch: I went into the men's room to pee. I said hello to Splasher Wilking, who was obviously there for the same purpose. While standing next to one another, we exchanged some inane chitchat about the good old days when I was at Soona and he was my canoeing instructor. He told me the camp was even better today than when I went there and much more rugged in approach. I said that sounded terrific and I was sure Ben would get a heckuva lot out of the summer . . . it would really put hair on his chest. (Little did I know!) Then he asked wasn't I just a smidgeon jealous of my son, who was about to embark on this wonderful experience, and I said . . . well, I can't remember exactly what I said (my mind was three thousand miles away on how glad I was my secretary Madeline had booked me into the Beverly Hills instead of the Bel Air), but I *think* I said something on the order of how I'd give anything to be in his shoes—which I didn't even mean, I was only being *gracious!* But then, without so much as a violin sting, or a ripple of ascending notes on an electronic synthesizer—without any warning *whatsoever,* I was in the main waiting room of the Port Authority, in my son's brand-new desert boots, to say nothing of his skin, eyeball to eyeball with a child I'd never seen before in my life. Or if I had, I didn't remember.

Time out for digression: It was next to impossible to keep track of Ape Face's friends, he had such a slew of them. Small wonder, actually. He was a great little kid—top grades in school, held his own reasonably well in sports, never gave us a moment's trouble at home—and his instinctive response to any situation was always so considerate and generous, it could make an ordinary person—me for instance—feel about one inch tall. Ironically enough, he seemed to worship the ground I walked on—trotted around after me being politely deferential as though I were a minor deity—which made communication between us somewhat sticky. After all, how do you rap with a saint who thinks you're one? Answer: You don't. But that's neither here nor there.

More to the point is how do you rap with a twelve-year-old son who is poaching on your corporeal preserve (and crushing your best lightweight trousers in the bargain)? Accuse him of interloping? Call him a rotten body snatcher? Treat him with sweet reasonableness?—"I say, old sport, let's make a deal: I'll give you back your body if you'll give me back mine." Out of the question, unfortunately. In the first place, judging by the fatuous smile on his (my) face, he was perfectly contented with things as they now stood. (Still on one foot, crushing my trousers.) And in the second place, since I had no idea how we'd gotten ourselves into this unbelievable predicament, I was equally in the dark as to how we were going to get out.

In the meantime, there was at least one thing I could do. "Ape Face," I asked, "is that you?"

"Yes and no," he said coyly. For a forty-four-year-old man with a beard, coyly is not an appropriate way to respond.

"This is no time for tomfoolery," I told him, in a stern but squeaky voice. "Once again, is that you?"

"Yes."

"Then take my shoe off my best pants and stand properly!" I snapped.

"Whoops, sorry," he said, complying instantly. That was more like it!

"Come on, let's go somewhere where we can talk," I said, leading the way out of the men's room. "There's a coffee shop type place right here in the building."

"Okay," said Ape Face, striding after me. "But we'll have to talk fast—there isn't too much time."

With relish, he activated the dial on my $300 digital watch. "Nine-sixteen and thirty seconds. The bus leaves at nine-forty. You wouldn't want to miss it."

I stopped dead in my tracks. "Bus?! Are you kidding? You really think I'm going to climb on that Trailways torture chamber while you take off first class in a 747 for L.A.? What are you, crazy?!"

"No," he said, serene as a morning in May, "I'm not crazy, I'm you. And you"—pause, pause, pause—"are me."

So much for sainthood. The kid was getting more obnoxious by the minute. We walked the rest of the way in stony silence. Correction: The stony silence part is accurate. As for walking, neither of us walked. I trotted and sprinted, my puny legs pumping furiously to keep up with his long ones. And he? Well, first he hopped on one foot, then on the other; next, he hopped backward—into an old lady with an aluminum walker, which didn't faze him in the slightest (luckily, no damage done); then he skipped for a few yards; and for the fourth down, he gave himself a good running start, and slid on my Gucci loafers right into the revolving door. Have you ever seen a grown man in a beard and business attire hopping, skipping, and sliding in the Port Authority terminal? It looks damn stupid.

"Sit down and behave yourself," I hissed under my breath as we reached the counter. "And don't twirl on your seat."

"Why not?"

"Because, dummy, you now weigh a hundred and fifty-five pounds, and if you get going too fast, the seat'll come off and spin you through the plate-glass window." A nasty thought occurred to me. "Leaving me locked in this fragile frame of yours forever." I shuddered.

Ape Face looked pensive. "Gee, that's right. Then you'd have to grow up all over again."

He pointed to a plastic-encased drink dispenser. "Can I have some of that red bubbly stuff and a jelly doughnut?"

"Miss!" I called out, rapping impatiently on the napkin box with a saltshaker.

The waitress turned around and glared at me. "Yes, *sir*," she said with elaborate sarcasm. "What can I *do* for you, sir?"

"One black coffee, one jelly doughnut, and one raspberry bilge from your fountain of perpetual poison." If she could get snarky, so could I.

"Coming right up," she said, slapping the coffee in front of Ape Face and the bilge and the doughnut in front of me.

"No, the other way around," said Ape Face. Hands on hips, disbelief on face, she watched while he switched beverages, taking care not to spill in the process, and helped himself to an obscenely large bite of doughnut. "I let my son have whatever he wants," he announced with his mouth full.

"I can see that," she said sourly. "Is there anything else your son wants? A cigar, perhaps? Or an Alka-Seltzer for his tiny dyspeptic tummy? Because if not, that'll be a dollar fifteen."

Accustomed to my grabbing the check, Ape Face just sat there.

"Pay the lady, will you, Ape?"

He fumbled around in my pocket, finally came up with a handful of loose change, and deposited a dollar fifteen on the counter.

"Tip!" I muttered under my breath.

"How much?" he muttered back.

"Twenty percent."

Ape Face added exactly twenty-three cents.

"Thanks *ever* so!" said the waitress, and in search of more remunerative quarry flounced off to another customer.

Alone at last! And not a minute too soon. According to the Timex on my (his) wrist, the bus left in ten minutes.

"Now, listen, Ape Face," I said to my son the father, "let's get one thing straight. I don't know how this happened, but you are to tell no one about it. *No one,* do you understand?"

"How come?" He seemed surprised.

"How come? Because the whole business is so utterly,

outlandishly preposterous, people would think you were stark raving mad, that's how come. A hallucinating paranoid schizophrenic is what they'd figure you for, and the little men in the white coats would lock you up for life in the cookie jar. Is that what you want?"

"No!!" he gasped, paling under the beard.

"Well, then, not a word to a soul."

He sighed. "Not even Duck?"

"Not even *anyone*. . . . Who's Duck?"

"Duck is Duck Levine. My best friend."

"You have a best friend called Duck?!" Fascinating!

"That's not his real name. He's called Duck on account of he walks like one." More and more fascinating.

"Does he also quack like one?"

Ape Face shlurped the last of the raspberry bilge and shook his head. "Nope. Walks like a duck but sings like a bird. In choirs and operas and stuff. Last Christmas, he sang *Amahl and the Night Visitors* all over Long Island, and one performance in assembly at school. They call him the Jewish Nightingale."

"*Who* does?" I asked, aghast. Bigotry at Barden!

"His parents. It's okay, they're Jewish, too," he reassured me. Warming to the topic, he continued. "It's lucky he's in your bunk, because you're going to love Duck. He's very mature and sophisticated for his age."

That brought me up short. Bunk, shmunk!

"Ape Face . . ."

"Hmmn?" He was busy dropping water on a straw snake.

"Ben, pay attention!" That did it.

"What?"

I chose my words judiciously. "Ben, every little boy in the world wonders how it's going to feel to be all grown up like his father, with a deep voice, and hair on his chest, et cetera, et cetera . . ." Ape Face grinned sheepishly. Enough said about that. ". . . and I can easily imagine how uniquely exhilarating this . . . ah . . . switch, shall we call it, must be for you. Because now you *are* all grown up, right?"

He nodded happily.

"WRONG!" I shouted, pounding my fist on the counter for emphasis. "You are *not* all grown up, you only *look* all grown up. You are only a little boy . . . with jelly in your beard!" I added contemptuously. With a wet paper napkin I scrubbed vigorously at his face—never mind what the waitress thought as long as she couldn't hear me; then I lowered my voice to a hoarse whisper, and continued. "You are a little boy in what amounts to a furnished sublet, in temporary possession of *my* body, *my* clothes, *my* watch, *my* money, and credit cards and checkbook, and as soon as I can figure out how to do it, I'm going to evict you and get on with my life. But in the meantime"—I hopped off the seat, Ape Face followed suit—"here's what's going to happen. We're going to find your mother and tell her that you have decided to take me with you to California because I've changed my mind, and I don't want to go to camp after all."

"But," said Ape Face, as hand in hand, we started walking back to our group, "I thought you loved camp."

"Ape Face," I sighed, "are you being dense on purpose, or dense because you're dense?! Let me tell you something. As a result of the recent takeover at Galaxy Films, Ty Donovan, President of Worldwide Production and the man responsible for my being where I am today, has resigned. In his place is a woman—"

"Oh, good," said Ape Face, "Mom'll approve of that."

". . . a woman," I continued doggedly, "who is known in the company as a shark in sheep's clothing."

"So?" said Ape Face.

"So you're an imaginative little chap. What kind of a person does that sound like to you?"

"Not exactly a pussycat," said Ape Face.

"Very perceptive," I snapped. "It just so happens, according to everything I hear, the new boss *is* a pussycat—on the surface, that is, and devastatingly attractive, too; but underneath, she's the coldest fish in filmdom. And since her opinion of me may well determine the outcome of my entire career, I'm sure you can understand why I'm just the teensiest bit reluctant to entrust *you*" (a long beat, accompanied by a disdainful stare) "with the sole responsibility of making that vitally important first impression. Like it or not, buddy, I am coming with you. Is that clear?"

"Okay, I guess" was the meek response. And that solved that. Or so I thought. . . .

At the farthermost fringe of the Soonawissakit cluster, we finally located Ellen, anxiously searching for a glimpse of her wayward menfolk.

Before I could stop him, Ape Face crept up behind her and put his hands over her eyes. "Betcha don't know who this is," he said, winking broadly at me.

"Betcha I do," she said in a bored tone. (Oh, yeah!?) "Where were you anyway? I was beginning to worry."

"Me, too," said a familiar voice to my left.

I turned, and once again found myself eyeball to eyeball with . . .?, now, however, a furtive glance at . . .?'s feet told me all I needed to know. They were resolutely in fifth position—Pavlova herself couldn't have done it better.

So delighted was I at having solved the mystery of his identity, I promptly forgot my own.

"Hey!" I crowed triumphantly. "You must be Duck!" A fishy stare from Duck and onward I plunged. "I'd like you to meet my dad. Dad, this is Duck, Duck, this is Dad."

"We've met," said Ape Face with another giant wink.

"We *have?*" said Duck. By now, he probably thought we were both crazy.

A counselor toward the front of the group blew a whistle and delivered preliminary embarkation instructions. The troops were clearly on the move—it was now or never.

I tugged at the sleeve of Ape Face's (my) blazer.

"Tell her," I urged. *"Now."*

"Tell me what, darling?" asked Ellen, an unsuspecting smile on her face.

"Um," said Ape Face, his eyes on mine, his left loafer inching up his right leg (oh, nuts—there goes the other side

24

of my pants). "The thing is, I've changed my mind about wanting to go to camp—"

Dunderhead, fool, idiot, lamebrain—he couldn't remember who he was either!

I interrupted him with a dirty look and a cleverly ambiguous one-word hint: "Dad!"

He got the gist. "Hold it, hold it!" he demanded, lickety-split abandoning the stork stance. "Let me begin again."

"By all means, do," said Ellen.

This time he made it safely, though cautiously, through the whole speech, deliberately stressing each correct pronoun while simultaneously pointing to its rightful owner. To wit:

"*I* have decided to take *him* (Ben, that is), to California with *me* (his Dad), because *he* has changed his mind about wanting to go to camp. Haven't you, uh, Son." A nice but inaccurate final touch; I've never called him Son in my life.

"Oh, no!" wailed Duck, profoundly depressed at the prospect of an Ape-less four weeks. "You can't! You just can't!"

"That's right, he can't," agreed Ellen.

"Why can't I?" asked my son, the father.

"Because," said Ellen, "aside from the fact that it's utter lunacy for everything to be switched around at the last minute," you're telling me, dollface! "there are one or two practical considerations. Such as what are you going to do with him when you get back from California if I'm still in Window Rock, Arizona, with the Navajos—take him to the office with you every day?"

"Boy, that'd be neat!" exclaimed Ape Face.

"Funny, you've never thought so before, Bill," she said. "And another thing, I've already paid the camp—with *my* money, and it's too late to get a refund."

"Oh, well," I said with a blithe snap of the fingers, "easy come, easy go." It was a monstrous tactical error. Hell hath no fury like a feminist scorned.

She wheeled on me, ablaze with indignation. "Young man, I worked darn hard for that money, darn hard indeed. Don't you 'easy come, easy go' me!"

"No offense intended," I assured her. She dismissed me with a curt nod and renewed her attack on Ape Face.

"As for you, Bill, sweetheart, what on earth possessed you to make this half-baked, unilateral decision in the first place? I mean, instead of letting your son spend a nice, healthy, cool summer in Maine, with plenty of wholesome food and fresh air and exercise and sleep—"

At this juncture, to register my low opinion of the bucolic life, I interjected an inspired imitation of someone in a Grade B movie being strangled by a mobster. Ape Face snickered. My wife ignored both of us and, after a brief recap, plowed implacably on.

"Seriously, Bill, instead of a nice, cool camp in Maine, you want to drag that poor child all the way to California so he can choke to death on smog?! What kind of crummy summer is that for a twelve-year-old boy?!"

Traumatized by the onslaught, Mr. Nimble Wits chewed a hefty chunk out of the cuticle on my right thumb, and said,

"Gee, Mom, I guess you're right."

Wrong, wrong, wrong! I screamed silently. Suddenly everything was going wrong, and now the head counselor—who looked for all the world like your run-of-the-mill, beer-bellied, pig-eyed, sadistic Kommandant from Bergen-Belsen—was shouting final embarkation instructions, and the hordes were moving forward, and my time was running out! And so was my luck!...

Decision: I would stage a scene. Improvement: a *Scene*. Further improvement: a SCENE.

With a Rumpelstiltskin-like stamp of my desert boot, I bellowed, "I don't wanna, I don't wanna, I'm not gonna, nobody can make me, no*body,* no *way!* I'd rather be dead of a fulminating brain tumor!"—crude but effective, I thought, and flung myself into Ellen's arms, sobbing piteously. "Please, Mom, pretty please, pretty Mommy, puleeze don't make me!"

It was a pyrotechnical display of unsurpassed brilliance; and Ellen, whose compliant younger child could usually be counted on to behave with suitable decorum, was aghast.

"Good Lord, Bill, what do I do now?" she asked Ape Face.

"You don't do anything, Ma'am, *we* do it," said Splasher Wilking.

What "we" did was the ultimate humiliation. "We" picked me up, slung me over his shoulder like a duffel bag of dirty laundry, and carried me, wailing and flailing and upside down, toward the Trailways departure gate.

"Wait, I have to kiss Daddy good-bye!" I screamed.

"Bull diddly!" said Wilking, purposefully accentuating his already nautical swagger. We were yawing and pitching like a dinghy on the high seas; in a second, I might vomit down his back. That'd teach him!

"Daddy, come say good-bye!"

Ape Face, ever obedient and fleet of foot, quickly caught up with us. Then, upon realizing that communication with a perilously bobbing, upturned human duffel would be next to impossible, he adroitly adjusted his posture to accommodate mine—by running backward alongside me with his head tilted at an angle I never knew anyone but a freak-show contortionist was capable of achieving.

"Good-bye," he said breathlessly. "I hope you have a terrifically good time."

Wilking flashed him a look of contempt, and tightened his grip on my ankles. "What's the matter, Andrews—no little last kiss for Junior Miss?"

Ape Face dutifully lurched sideways in the general direction of my forehead.

"Never mind *that*," I croaked. We were practically there. I had roughly thirty seconds in which to impart a ton of vital information. Obviously, selectivity was the name of the game.

"Listen, *call* me! Promise you'll call me as soon as you get to the Beverly Hills Hotel. That's the Bev-er-ly Hills. In Beverly Hills. Don't forget your credit cards and your briefcase, the ticket's in the briefcase—TWA, five-o'clock flight, Kennedy—and about driving, you know how they drive in

California—like maniacs!. . . So unless you want to get killed on the Santa Monica Freeway or lost halfway down the Baja Peninsula where a bunch of Mexican bandits will rob you blind, don't ever get behind the wheel of a car. I want your solemn word on that! Do I have your solemn word?"

It was just at this crucial point that Splasher Wilking reached the narrow doorway leading to the outside ramp. Without a moment's hesitation, he plunged through it, while Ape Face, also without a moment's hesitation, backed smack into the wall of the terminal.

As for the solemn word, I couldn't quite catch it, but I think it was "Awp!"

Three

"Awp!" I said, caroming off the wall and pitching flat on my face on the floor.

In their mad rush to get on the bus, all kinds of campers stepped over and around me; one, a klutz in cleats (anyway, it felt like cleats), even stepped *on* me; and one—out of about fifty or so kids, one only!—bothered to help me up.

"Are you all right, sir?" asked good old Duck in a concerned voice.

"Absolutely, thank you, Duck." I managed a weak laugh. "That's what I get for not looking where I'm going, ha-ha-ha!" Ha-ha-ha! in your hat if you think there's anything funny about a mashed hand and a matching pair of bruised kneecaps.

"Well, okay then, if you're sure," said Duck, inching toward the door. "Because Ape Face and I agreed to sit together on the bus and I wouldn't want him to think I was a no-show, especially in the mood he's in, if you follow me."

"Duck, you're a good friend," I told him. "And

don't worry, Ape Face is going to be just fine."

"Boy, I hope you're right. For my sake as well as his," he added uneasily. "You see, all along I've been kind of counting on him to keep my spirits up, but the way he's been acting today—all that screaming and yelling and nut stuff . . ." Perplexed, he combed his fingers through a hunk of long blond hair. "Gee, Mr. Andrews, do you think he's having a nervous breakdown?—because that's just not the Ape Face I know!"

I considered leveling with him ("Curious you should mention that, Duck. It just so happens he's in my body and I'm in his." "Golly! You must be a hallucinating paranoid schizophrenic! Wait right here; I'll go call the little men in the white coats."), then thought better of it.

"True," I admitted truthfully. "But cheer up, this can't last forever." How truthful was *that*? I wondered. Maybe it could. Would . . . wow!. . . weird . . .

Out of the corner of my eye, I saw a few final stragglers being herded through the door by Mr. Mallison, one of the counselors. (And was sinfully glad not to be one of them.)

"Well, I guess you'd better get going, Duck. Listen, if I get a chance on the Coast, I'll send you some long-life batteries for your transistor."

He looked around guiltily. Radios weren't allowed at Soonawissakit. He probably wondered how come I knew he was sneaking one in.

31

"Sh," he cautioned, finger to lips, then gave me a grateful hug and bolted for the bus.

"Don't worry," I shouted after him, "Ape Face is going to be just fine, absolutely terrifically fine. He will, I promise!"

Maybe it was just a case of saying is believing, but all of a sudden I was filled with this wonderful sense of pride and confidence in myself. And I don't mean my superficial Bill self (although it certainly doesn't hurt to be over six feet tall, dark, and handsome, with hair on your chest and other places, a deep, commanding voice, and money in your pocket), I mean my inner Ape Face self.

Suddenly I knew that I, Benjamin Ape Face Andrews, former Yellow Jell-O champion of the world, would inherit the earth, and the sky . . . and the entire West Coast office of Galaxy Films.

As for poor little piddling William Waring Andrews, "Well, too bad for you," I said to myself jubilantly, and marched off to find my mother—*wife*.

Four

"He wanted me to tell you not to worry, everything was going to be just fine."

Oh, yeah? I turned my back and stared out the bus window. All those glum-faced people walking around free as air on Tenth Avenue, not appreciating their good fortune—it was enough to make you cry.

"And another thing he said, Ape Face . . . Ape Face, are you listening?"

"Unh?" I grunted, back still turned.

"He said he'd try to send me some transistor batteries when he got to the Coast. What Coast?"

"West Coast."

"What's he doing on the West Coast? I thought he was in advertising in New York. On the Glamour Gums account."

"That was years ago. He's in films, now. Anyway, it's gams."

"What?"

"Gams," I corrected him irritably. "Not gums, gams . . . Glamour *Gams*." Jackass kid!

"Are you sure?" he persisted. "I always thought it was

toothpaste. Are you sure it wasn't toothpaste? Or a dentifrice?"

"Panty hose!" I bellowed. "Glamour *Gams,* made out of Clingalon, the fabulous new fashion fabric that conforms to your figure and is guaranteed never to bag, wrinkle, or run, is *panty hose,* and I ought to know!"

The entire bus erupted in raucous laughter. A red-faced, red-haired, green-eyed, green-toothed slob leered over the back of the seat in front of me and lisped, "Ith that tho!"

More raucous laughter, followed by several lewd whistles and a foxtrot demonstration in the aisle, mincingly executed and sung ("Yeth, Thir, That'th My Baby") by two fourteen-year-old scions of the country-club set.

"Siddown and shuddup!" Splasher Wilking thundered at them. "As for you," he said, wagging a menacing finger under my nose, "if I hear another word out of you, another single sissy syllable, I'll throw you off the bus in White Plains!"

Wonderful! Less than ten minutes into the summer and already everybody had my son pegged as a hotheaded homo with a penchant for ladies' lingerie. Maybe getting thrown off the bus wasn't such a bad idea.

"Is that a promise, Cap'n?" I asked hoping against hope.

Regrettably, it was merely an idle threat.

Five

WHAT EVERY TWELVE-YEAR-OLD BOY MAS-
QUERADING AS A GROWN-UP OUGHT TO
KNOW ABOUT TRAVEL BUT SHOULDN'T
ASK—unless he's prepared to be taken for an imbe-
cile.

This is a list of helpful hints, based on incidents that
occurred during the next few hours of my life. To anyone tempted to skip reading it—on the assumption
that he'll never find himself in the body of his father
anyway—all I can say is I think that's a pretty reckless
assumption. After all, I never thought it would happen
to me.

On Being Lost

If you can't find your wife/mother in the Port
Authority Bus Terminal, what should you do?

a) Break out in a cold sweat because suddenly you're
all alone?

b) Ask the man at the Information booth if he's seen
your mother—an attractive, medium-tall, brown-eyed,

brown-haired lady . . . about thirty-nine years old? (Completely forgetting that you look older than that yourself.)

c) Figure, after fifteen minutes of concerted searching, that she's gone home without you, and go home as fast as you can—in a taxi?

d) None of the above.

The answer is: None of the above. I did all of the above, except d), of course—and when Mom finally got home, twenty minutes after me, she was in a foul mood.

There are three lessons to be learned from all of this. The first is that when it comes to desertion in grubby public places, grown-ups don't react any better than kids.

"Thanks a lot," Mom said bitterly. "You should just try being a defenseless woman surrounded by nothing but hoods and harlots sometime, and see how you like it!" Thanks a lot yourself, lady, I've already got my hands full trying to be a middle-aged man.

"Sorry, babes"—Dad occasionally calls her babes. Whenever possible, emulate the speech patterns of your alter ego—it lends verisimilitude—"but I thought you'd left."

"Left! When did I ever?!"

Which brings me to the second lesson. A grown-up doesn't usually desert you without any warning; so even though the grown-up seems to have vanished into thin air, do not expect the worst. She is probably in the bathroom, fixing her lipstick. At least, that's where Mom was.

The third lesson has to do with cabdrivers and big bills. When a driver tells you he is not obliged by law to leave his cab to make change for you, and you are not permitted by law to leave his cab until you have paid him, "Therefore, if you don't got nothing smallern a twenny, you gotta gimme the twenny, irregardless," that driver is lying in his teeth. This is a perfect example of being taken for an imbecile. Also for a ride.

Packing

If you're going to be away for two weeks, don't forget to take a suitcase with some stuff, or your wife/mother will think you're a real oddball. I know mine did.

"Bill, your plane leaves in an hour and a half. Hadn't you better get started?"

"If you say so, my love," I said, giving her a peck on the cheek and heading for the front door. "Good-bye, see you on Soonawissavisitors' Day—July sixteenth, isn't it?"

"I mean get started packing," she said, looking at me strangely.

"Good Lord!" I slapped my forehead with the palm of my hand. "It slipped my mind altogether."

"Maybe your mind is slipping altogether," she suggested dryly. Not slipping, merely on the move, I was tempted to say. (Attention: Resist all such temptations; they do not lend verisimilitude.)

Okay, now for the packing itself. This can be a somewhat tricky business. You may not know which stuff your Dad would want to take or where it is, or even where the suitcase is, and you also may not know how to do the actual packing because your mother has always done it for you. The safest stratagem is to let her do it for you again—although, these days, that takes a certain amount of manipulating.

"Honey, if you're not too busy, how would you like to throw a few things in a bag for me?"

A quizzical look, followed by, "What am I—your slave?"

A stricken look, followed by "Golly, Ellen, how insensitive can a fellow get! You must think I have some nerve, asking a favor like that of you!"

An incredulous look, followed by a burst of good-natured laughter, followed by, "Oh come on now, Willy, it's hardly a federal offense!" followed by the rapid selection of an appropriate California wardrobe, followed by the deft placing of same in a hanging garment bag and a medium-large piece of Samsonite . . . and ta-da, what do you know—that was that in no time flat!

Finally, if, at the last minute, you decide you can't live without your collection of *Lampoons,* your *Find the Hidden Words* paperback puzzle book, and the pink plush hippo you've kept your pajamas in ever since Uncle Burt gave it to you for your sixth birthday, that's okay. Just make sure you hide these things at the bottom of the suitcase where your wife won't see them when she goes to put in the toenail clippers she forgot; because if she does see them she'll probably ask scornfully, "What in heaven's name is all this?" and you won't know what to answer.

For me, that particular problem never came up; I hid everything in my briefcase. For some reason or other, women never open men's briefcases. I guess they think it's rude.

Departures

You may be edgy about getting there on your own, but don't invite your wife to come with you to the airport; you'll discover she hasn't done this in years. "It's not that I don't love you, Bill darling, but I've seen an airport. Besides, I have my own packing to do." If you're lucky, you'll find some other tenant (in my case, a Mrs. Herman Wormser from 11F) waiting in front of your building for a cab to Kennedy, and dying to share it with you. If not, relax; the cabdriver will know a million ways to get there. One of them, according to Mrs. Wormser, a seasoned traveler, is via Westchester County, takes over two hours, and costs fifty-two bucks, minus tip. Needless to say, this is not the best route. The Triborough Bridge is the best route, because when you say to the driver in an authoritative tone, "Kennedy Airport, take the Triborough," he figures you know where you're going and doesn't dare mess around. Anyway, that's what Mrs. Wormser did, and it worked.

At the Airport

TWA, on a Saturday, is a very busy place. The clerk behind the check-in counter and all the people behind you in line won't like to be kept waiting while you fumble in six different pockets for the plane ticket—or, if you're me, surreptitiously rummage around for it under the pink hippo in your briefcase. And when asked whether you prefer smoking or nonsmoking, try to refrain from hooting with mirth; remember, adults consider this a perfectly sensible question. In other words, A.Y.A.*!

On the Plane

First class is different from tourist. As soon as you sit down they offer you stuff: newspapers and magazines— they won't have *Penthouse,* so don't bother to ask; free headsets—if it's one of those Disney flicks about a talking woodchuck at Michigan State, A.Y.A. and don't accept—you'd be the only one watching; they'll also offer you a free preflight champagne cocktail. Don't

---

* Act Your Age

accept that either—it'll go to your head and loosen your tongue—next thing you know you'll be yackety-yacketing with your seatmate.

Her name was Peggotty Horn. Fiftyish, fattish, and friendly. Tan leather bag, tan leather shoes, tan leather skin, hair of honey and a voice to match.

"So you're with Galaxy Films, Mr. Andrews," she enthused mellifluously during hors d'oeuvres. "I hear they've had quite a shake-up over there. Care to tell me about it?"

"Wuh, ashually . . ." Due to something rubbery and disgusting in my mouth, I was coming through muffled. Swallow first, talk later, I figured. "Nuhshing mushatell."

"Excuse me?" she inquired.

Chomp, chomp, chomp—the stuff just wouldn't go down. "Whash *izh*-ish?!" I said desperately, pointing at my plate.

"Come again?" said Peggotty.

"Mediterranean Fruits de Mer," said a passing flight attendant, who understood perfectly. "Mussels, clams, scallops, and squid in a flavorful garlic—"

"Urghh!" I moaned. The flight attendant understood that, too.

"Here, sir," she said, hastily handing me a glass of water. Gulp, gulp, gulp, the day was saved. I thanked her, and turned back to Peggotty.

"You were saying?" she prompted. What *was* I

saying? Between the champagne and the Fruits de Mer, I'd kind of lost track.

"About the shake-up."

"Ah, yes. Well, let me see now. Ty Donovan resigned—"

"Resigned? Oh, come off it, baby cakes, what're you giving me?" she purred. "Ty Donovan didn't resign, Ty Donovan was canned; otherwise, how come that item about him ankling to Indie Prod, right, baby cakes?" She kiss-kissed at me and continued the inquest. "Now what about Stephanie Marshak—" Stephanie Marshak? Indie Prod? Who *were* all these people!

"You tell me," I suggested cleverly.

"Listen, I didn't meet her yet, but anyone who goes from lowly script girl to first female president of a film company in five short years," oh, *her!* "is either very smart or very, *very*"—she gazed knowingly at me—"alluring, if you know what I mean."

"Both. Definitely both," I assured her. And then, between forkfuls of Tender Prime Ribs of Beef au Jus and Potatoes Anna (the Broccoli Mornay, I passed up), I verbatimed what Dad had said about the devastatingly attractive shark in sheep's clothing, pussycat on the surface, coldest fish in filmdom, et cetera, et cetera, blah-blah-blah, ending up with an inspired invention of my own.

"And you'll never guess what her nickname is."

"Tell, *tell!*" begged Peggotty, all agog.

At that point we were interrupted by a flight attendant with the dessert cart asking what we wanted on our sundaes. I said everything; Peggotty, impatient to get on with it, said nothing, just plain vanilla.

"So what *do* they call her, baby cakes? I'm dying of suspense!"

A nice long pause while I loaded up my spoon with a huge gob of butterscotch, tilted my head back, and dribbled it into my mouth from above.

"Strictly off the record," pleaded Peggotty.

"The Killer Cream Puff!" I announced. "Isn't that great?!"

"Fabulous!" she gurgled. "Simply fabulous. Who's responsible for that one, I wonder."

"Me," I said smugly, licking butterscotch remnants off the back of my spoon.

"Well, *you,*" she said, "are nothing short of di*vine!*" Then she curled up against the window and went to sleep. Which reminds me: In first class, you can get seconds on dessert, so instead of letting the flight attendant catch you stealing your seatmate's dish of melting vanilla, just ask for another butterscotch sundae. She'll be happy to oblige. Also, don't forget to use your napkin or some kid on his way back from the bathroom will stop by your seat to tell you you have nuts in your mustache.

Other helpful don'ts are: Don't practice your

father's signature in public unless you've prepared a logical explanation for this. I told the man across the aisle I was trying to get the ink flowing in my ballpoint, but when he noticed the American Express card I was copying from, it made him kind of suspicious, I think.

Finally, don't fall asleep reading the Galaxy production "book" containing thirty or so pages of highly confidential info about present and future film projects. Because when you wake up just in time to prevent Peggotty Horn from ever so gently slipping it off your lap and onto her own, you'll be too dumb to worry about what if she'd succeeded. That's because you're too dumb to know who she is. (More about that later.)

Six

"God bless our home away from home
And help us do our bit
To cherish every stick and stone
Of Soonawissakit,"

warbled the Soonawissakiddies as they eagerly tumbled out of the bus.

Duck and I, last off, stood to one side in a desolate huddle. Up ahead, someone with a clipboard and a bullhorn was barking instructions we were too nervous to listen to, much less assimilate.

"How's it look to you?" whispered Duck.

"I'd hoped for better. . . ." Any other camp would have made a few improvements in thirty years—enlarged the dining hall, bulldozed the rocks out of the ballfield, upgraded the washroom facilities, or at least painted the dock a different color—"But it's exactly the same," I observed.

"As what?" asked Duck.

"As it always was," I said, reminiscing gloomily. "Ice-cold

showers, moldy tents, black flies, spiders, bloodsuckers . . . *bats!. . .*" suddenly it was all coming back with horrendous clarity, "not to mention the kid who snored, the kid who wet his bed every night and had to sleep in garbage bags . . . and the constant rain—it must've rained thirty out of the forty-nine da—"

Duck clutched my arm. "Ape Face, if your dad told you all that," but I hadn't, of course, having only just remembered it, "why are we here? Why did you want to come?"

Good question. All I ever said to Ape Face was if he wanted to go to my old camp, that was fine with me—hardly a rave review.

"Good question," I said.

Duck grabbed me by the neck of my Soonawissakitee-shirt. "Listen, scum, you told me he said it was wonderful!"

"Obviously, *he** was lying!"

"Shaddup!" growled a voice from behind. "I'm trying to hear what cabin I'm in, so just shaddup!" A sharp blow between the shoulder blades knocked me into the guy in front, who without bothering to turn around retaliated with an elbow gouge in my ribs.

"Charming chap," I muttered to Duck, sneaking a peek at the guy in back. To my no great surprise, it was the same red-haired, green-eyed, green-toothed slob who'd made fun of me on the bus.

---

* The Ambiguous He, a device akin to the Editorial We, but much more useful to someone in my predicament.

"What do you expect from Hitzigger? He hates you."
Does he now?

"Why is that?" I asked.

"I don't know. He's always hated you." Duck continued
bitterly, "Listen, count your blessings, he's the only one. A lot
of people hate me."

"De Menocal, Swensen, Biddle, Beaty, and King will be
quartered in High Ledge with Snorkel Bains," bellowed the
bullhorn. "And with Mr. Mallison in Mount Olympus," a mis-
nomer if I ever heard one; Mount Olympus is a damp dump,
"Murdock, Andrews, Levine, Von Volkening, and Hitzigger."

"Ke-ristmas! Gimme a break!" yelped Hitzigger. "If my
old man knew I was rooming with a singing faggot and a
panty-hose queen, he'd have me home in no time."

"That'd be hunky-dory with us," retorted Duck, where-
upon Hitzigger promptly knocked him to the ground, and I,
committing the ultimate betrayal, played the role of a disin-
terested bystander. (Not that I wanted to, you understand.
My natural inclination was to clobber the Bejeezus out of
Hitzigger, but trapped as I was in the body of my noncom-
bative son, there was a good chance Hitzigger would clobber
me instead, thus contributing yet another black mark to Ape
Face's already besmirched reputation which he/I could ill
afford.)

"Here," I said, offering Duck a hand up.

"It's okay," said Duck, rising unassisted to his splayed
feet. "Not that I expected you to defend me physically or
anything," was this a mild rebuke or wasn't it? "but the next

time it happens, maybe you could shout one of your usual *No! No!*s or *Don't* DO *that!*s. It might've helped."

"The next time it happens, it won't happen," I declared, "because just let him lift one little finger at either of us, I'm gonna bust that s.o.b. right in the chops!"

"That'll be the day," said Duck with a tolerant smile. "That'll really be the day."

Seven

Question: What's big and pink and sprawls all over?
Answer: The Beverly Hills Hotel.

According to Dad, the Bev Hills is beyond compare. Well maybe, but according to me, you could compare it with a HoJo's and the latter would win hands down—except for outside appearances. (All HoJo's look the same—if you hate one orange roof, you hate them all. On the other hand, pink is a really dumb color for a hotel, so I guess you could call it a tie.)

Here's what goes on at the Bev Hills: If your plane arrives at 7:40 (10:40 in New York), by the time the cab gets you to the hotel, it's almost nine. Then you check in at the desk, nervous about having to put your not-quite-perfected William W. Andrews signature on the registration card. Luckily, the reception guy says, "Charge it to the company, Mr. Andrews?" so that's no problem. What's slightly a problem is his handing you the key to your "Same old room, sir, the boy will be right along with the bags," because you don't even know your way to the elevator, let alone where to go when you get off it (assuming the room is not on the ground floor). This is solved by waiting for the "boy"—who's no more of a boy than I am (ha-ha!), he's a middle-aged man with a paunch—to lead you there. (Fourth floor, go right when you get out of the elevator down a long hall, left down another long hall, then right again, and into a fantastically huge corner room with a king-sized bed, wraparound terrace, color TV, flowers, and a basket of fruit from Richard de Virgilio. Who? Some friend of Dad's, probably.)

Now for another small problem. The "boy" won't leave. Hangs around doing stupid things like closing the curtains, adjusting the air-conditioning, turning on the lights in the closet and the bathroom, showing you how the television works (I *know* how a television works!), telling you there's a swimming pool and three tennis courts . . .

"Thank you, that's terrific," you say, tactfully opening the door for him.

"Thank *you* sir," he says, slamming the door behind him. Where have you heard that super-nice-on-the-surface, nasty-underneath voice before? you wonder. The waitress in the Port Authority coffee shop, you remember. *Tip!* you remember, and fish out a quarter—but it's too late. He's already out of sight. Oh well, you can give it to him tomorrow.

Here's a bigger problem. It's now about 9:45 (12:45

in New York) and you should be tired but you're not. After sampling two grapes and half a pink-and-slimy something-or-other (mango? papaya?), you realize you're not hungry either. What you are is bored.

You open the briefcase and take a look at the Week-at-a-Glance datebook under Thurs., June 30; maybe there's a big Hollywood party you're supposed to go to. There isn't. TV's no good either—nothing but reruns.

You might as well unpack. Flat stuff in the drawers, hanging stuff in the closet, the pants you've been wearing (and storking on) in a ball on the floor—they need pressing anyway. Then you take your pajamas out of the pink hippo and start to get into them, but surprise, surprise! they don't fit because they're not yours, idiot, they're *his*. So you put the hippo back in the briefcase, wondering where are yours, then?

Standing in your nude, searching one drawer after another, you decide Mom forgot to pack them. Either that or Dad doesn't wear any (woo-hoo! pretty racy for an old guy!). Possibly he sleeps in swimming trunks— not as fun a theory but more plausible, considering the two pairs of trunks in the bottom drawer. Hold it! you think, could be he *swims* in swimming trunks! That's what you'll do, that's exactly what you feel like doing! So you climb into the blue ones with the red stripe down the side, grab a towel, and head quick-o for the pool. You can hardly wait.

It's at about this point, folks, that you* . . . that *I* began to get disgusted with the good old Bev Hills that's so beyond compare, because the entrance to the pool was locked. A mistake, obviously.

Up the stairs to the lobby I sprinted (pant, pant, puff, puff; boy, Dad's in rotten shape—in my own body I could beat him in a race, easy!), and made my modest request to a lady busy shuffling papers behind the reception desk. "Listen, would somebody please do me a great favor and let me into the pool area, if it's not too much trouble?"

It was as polite as I knew how to make it, but in Hollywood, politeness is not the way to go, evidently. The lady didn't even bother to look up.

"Sorry, sir, the pool is closed," she said, flat out.

"What for?" Polluted?

"For the night."

"Aw, come on," I wheedled, "I'm all ready to go in!"

That got to her. She immediately stopped shuffling and frowned up at me.

"Well you shouldn't be," she said sternly. "The management doesn't consider swimming attire appropriate for the lobby. As you can see." She gestured toward gobs of people milling around, all of them very

---

* I don't know why I keep saying you, I don't mean you, I mean me.

52

dressed up (on their way to those parties I wasn't invited to, no doubt), and several of them staring at me.

Uncomfortable but determined, I stood stork and stood my ground. "Management is dead right. Swimming attire would be much more appropriate in a swimming pool. So how about—"

"Sir," she said through clenched teeth, "The management *does not permit swimming attire in this lobby is that clear!*"

"Want me to take it off?" I threatened. Kidding, of course, but if politeness isn't the way to go in Hollywood, neither is funnyness. She signaled with alarmed eyes to someone in back of me who smarmily inquired, "What seems to be the difficulty, Miss Vondermuhl?"

Uh-oh, here comes trouble, how would Dad handle it? With authority—cool and firm. FIRM. *Both* feet on the ground.

"That's what I'd like to know," I said, destorking and turning. Once again, I was face to face with a face that knew mine but I didn't know his.

"Why it's Mr. Andrews, welcome back!"

"Not so's you'd notice," I said coolly.

He looked me up and down, mostly down. Inadvertently, I storked (firm, *firm,* you fool!) then destorked.

"Your room is not satisfactory, sir?" Must be the manager.

"My room," I said with an impatient flick of the towel, "is perfectly fine. What's not so fine is your pool rule. *And* your dress code," I added for Vondermuhl's benefit.

"Mr. Andrews," he reasoned, "please don't be childish." (Yuk-yuk!) "If we let you wander around like that, we'd have to let everybody."

"Then couldn't you change your pool rule and I'll wander around in the water? What's the pool doing closed for the night for anyway?"

Not unaware of the small crowd of busybodies we were beginning to attract, he plowed pleasantly on. "Well for one thing, it gets cold in the evening and most of our guests don't care for swimming so late." Neither would I if I had a party to go to.

"It's colder and later in New York and we all swim there—I even swam in a HoJo's pool at midnight once, in Keene, New Hampshire. That was really cold!"

"Besides, we have no lifeguard on duty now," he added.

"So what, so *what*?!" I squealed. "I've got a Red Cross Advanced *Swimmers*, for crumb sake! Would you be happier if I wore a Styrofoam bubble?! Okay," I shouted, "who here wants to lend me their Styrofoam bubble?"

Apprehensively, the crowd backed off a few feet— you'd've thought I was the Hillside Strangler. To be fair, you could hardly blame them. I don't know how I look when I get mad because it happens so rarely and I'm never in front of a mirror when it does (who is?), but I know how Dad looks. Demented! This was no time for demented.

I adjusted the towel around my shoulders. "Couldn't we continue our discussion in a more private location?" I inquired loftily.

"Perhaps my office, sir" was his prompt suggestion.

"As you wish," I replied, and allowed myself to be deftly steered to a room behind the cashier's cubicle, where I settled myself cross-legged in an easy chair in front of the desk, and he perched on it (desk, not chair). Frankly, I was relieved to be off the hook.

So, apparently, was he. "I really do apologize," he said with an ingratiating smile, "but they're not my rules, you know."

"Yeah, I know," I conceded grudgingly, picking my left big toenail (a little habit I caught from Annabel which she recently broke herself of—to save the nail polish, I guess). "The thing is, what do you *do* around here?"

"Me? I work," he said wryly.

"No, no, not you, *me*. What do *I* do around here? Swimming is out, what else is there?"

He was puzzled. I elaborated. "Don't you have a game room—with a Space Invaders in it?" He shook his head. "Asteroids, then? Or Galaxia—it's not so good, but—" More head shaking, continuing throughout the next. "Pinball?. . . A pool table? No pool table?. . . *Darts!*. . . No?! Not even darts, well what *do* you have in your game room, nothing but cards, I'll bet," I said scornfully, "for silly old ladies to play bridge. Well, okay, you want to play me a game of Crazy Eights? I'll win, I usually do, maybe you'd rather play Double Solitaire?"

In a minute he was going to have himself a fat case of Inner Ear Disturbance from too much head shaking.

"What does *this* mean," I said, shaking my own head, "No, you don't want to play Crazy Eights or no, you don't want to play Double Solitaire? Or"—an incredible thought occurred to me—"no, you don't have any cards in there, either?"

One final shake, followed by a "you got it" nod of affirmation.

"You're kidding!" Outraged, I began a negative countdown. "No Space Invaders, no Asteroids, no Galaxia, no pool table, no pinball, no darts—"

"No game room."

"No cards, no— What did you say?! No *game* room?" Unbelievable!

Now it was his turn for a negative countdown. "That's correct," he said blandly. "No game room, and no Boom Boom room, and no discotheque—as a matter of fact, we don't even have a jukebox on the premises—"

"Well what am I supposed to do around here all night?" I demanded angrily. "Sit in my room smelling flowers and munching funny fruit sent by some total utter stranger?"

"Mr. Andrews," he protested, "we may not be bosom buddies, but I wouldn't exactly call me a total stranger."

A quick look at the i.d. sign on his desk confirmed it. Richard de Virgilio, Mgr. At the thought of hurting his feelings, I instantly reverted to type. (Yellow Jell-O.) "Heck, no, heck, *no!*" I heartily assured him. "And thank you so much. It was extremely generous of you."

"No, it wasn't," he said rather ungraciously. "The management pays and we send it to everyone." Thud.

After a weary sigh, he continued in a friendlier but baffled tone. "Mr. Andrews, what's gotten *into* you this trip?" (Wouldn't *you* like to know!) "You've been here many times before, you're familiar with us, you know which services we offer and which ones we don't. . . . Mr. Andrews, putting it very bluntly, we are not a Howard Johnson's."

"You said it, I didn't," I told him. "In my opinion, you are absolutely beyond compare!" He beamed complacently. I stood up, and on exiting, added, "With the possible exception of a morgue."

Thus endeth the Gospel According to Ape Face on the subject of HoJo versus the boring Beverly Hills Hotel. The rest of the night was less boring only because I slept through it in my king-sized bed—until five A.M. (eight A.M. in New York, also in Maine), when the phone rang.

Eight

"C'mon, 'mon, 'mon, answer the phone, why don't you!" I begged.

"Because he's asleep, creep," said Annabel.

"Eight o'clock, any right-thinkin' person's risin' and shinin'," grumbled Splasher Wilking.

The three of us were in the admin office above the dining room, where I had ingested a seven-hundred-and-fifty-calorie carbohydrate festival of o-juice, oatmeal, pancakes, sausages, and cocoa. (Under duress, you understand—a plea for "just plain toast and coffee, I can't eat all this" having elicited a short laugh from the counselor and "Eat it now when it's hot, or for lunch when it's not" in singsong unison from my fellow campers.)

"I'm sorry, sir, there seems to be no an—"

"Keep ringing," I told the operator. "Up, *up!*" I said into the phone.

"Face it, kid, your old man's the same city slugabed he always was."

"But Captain Wilking," said Annabel, hotly defending dear old Dad, "he's in California, where it's a lot earlier."

She flashed me a dirty look.

"Unh," groaned Ape Face, at last.

"Daddy," I began, "I'm sorry to wake you—"

"You're not waking me," mumbled Ape Face—which was confirmed instantly by the sound of heavy breathing.

"Hey!" I said.

"California!" Wilking poked me in the chest with his finger. "I want time and charges on this one, squirt!"

"Considering the thousand-dollar tab, I should think Soonawissakit could pop for one long-distance call," I told him.

"Ape Face!" Annabel was shocked.

"Aren't you kinda forgettin' yourself, young feller!" warned Wilking.

"Right." I shrugged apologetically and went back to the phone. "Ben!" I shouted. Wrong! A quick fix: "This is *Ben.* Your son Ben."

"Hi, Ben," murmured Ape Face. *Ben?* He knew perfectly well I wasn't Ben! Either he was extremely sleepy or . . .

"Is there someone in the room with you?" I asked, not realizing how peculiar this was going to sound.

"At five in the morning and Mom's in the desert?!" said Annabel, aghast. Wilking concentrated on filling his pipe.

"I just wondered," I said, opting for wide-eyed innocence—after all, what would a twelve-year-old child know about marital infidelity anyway?—"are you having a sleepover or something?"

"Dad!" said Ape Face. More than I thought. Well at least he was awake.

"Please, Daddy, this is important," I pleaded. "You've got to get me out of here. Because I need you, and *you . . . need . . . me,* believe me you do!"

"Oh, he does *not!*" said Annabel, thoroughly disgusted.

Wilking grabbed the phone out of my hand.

"But Daddy," said the phone on the way to Wilking's ear. We all three heard it. Two of us blinked. I winced.

"What's goin' on here anyhow?" Wilking asked me. "You call him Daddy, he calls *you* Daddy, hell's bells, let's all call him Daddy.

"Hey there, Daddy," he said into the phone, "this is Cap'n Splasher Wilking. Your youngun here's takin' himself a sorry spell a I dunno what, homesicketyness, most likely—says he didn't sleep a wink all night, and then this mornin' made such a ruckus at breakfast just now over wantin' to get you on the phone, his sister had to leave her own breakfast and drag him up here to do that."

He listened for a second. Then, in response to a seemingly irrelevant question, he looked at Annabel. "Is she mad? I dunno. Ask her yourself." He passed her the phone.

"I am not mad," said Annabel. "I am apoplectic with rage and humiliation. Dad, he's been a complete maniac ever since he got off the bus."

Wilking reclaimed the phone. "Shoulda seen him *on* the bus," he added. "And before. Hoo-ie!" Another brief listen, then, "Yup, I forgot, you did see him before, didn't you, Daddy. Well then, you know what I'm talkin' about." Chuckle, chuckle. "But never you mind, we'll shape him up in no time.

61

Meanwhile, anythin in partikler you want me to tell him?"

He listened, then repeated to me, "Don't worry . . . every-thin's fine . . . the hotel's fine . . . the plane ride was fine . . . he sat next to a nice lady called Peggotty Horn . . ."

Peggotty Horn! I made an adrenalin-fueled leap to Wilking's ear and grabbed the phone back. "You didn't talk to her, did you?"

"Sure I talked to her. It would've been rude not to. She was talking to me."

"No, no, no, what I mean is you didn't quote me on any-thing, did you—about business things, for instance?"

"Why?" said Ape Face cautiously.

"Because Peggotty Horn is the new show-biz gossip reporter on the *Today* show, that's why." Dunce! Clod!

"Ape Face, Dad knows how to take care of himself," said Annabel.

"*Did* you?" I repeated menacingly.

Silence from the phone. Flat on his back in bed, storking horizontally, I'll bet—and about to tell me a big fat lie.

"Uh, no, not really," said Ape Face. A big fat lie, I could hear it in his voice. By now, I was probably out of a job.

"Listen, you listen to me," I shouted. "Either you tell Captain Wilking to put me on the next available flight to the coast or I'll throw myself off a mountaintop and it'll be all your fault!" I thrust the phone at Wilking.

"Kid's talkin' hogwash, sir," drawled Wilking in a voice that would lull a lion. "Forty years Soonawissakit's been run-nin', we never had a suicide yet and we're not fixin' to have one now. So you can go on back to sleep with a clear conscience."

A look of disbelief, followed by "Nighty-night to you, too, sir," concluded the conversation.

Gently, he replaced the phone in the cradle, then, not so gently, gave me a knuckle rap on the head.

"I got one or two things to say to you, young feller. Thing one is your daddy, and me, and Sis, here, all agree . . ." without even knowing what she was agreeing to, "Sis, here," alias my daughter the fink, nodded heartily, "that you are stayin' in this camp whether you like it or no. Thing two is before you can throw yourself off a mountain, you gotta learn how to climb one."

He glanced at his watch. "The Outward Bound program— includin' rock scalin' and the like, begins in four minutes. See that he gets there," he barked to Annabel, and stomped out of the room.

Trapped. Helpless and trapped. Helpless, *jobless*, and trapped—with a wife and two children to support. Or an inaccessible mother, an unsympathetic sister, and a twelve-year-old father to depend on. Either way, it stank.

It's enough to make you cry! I said to myself. Out loud, apparently.

"Go ahead," said Annabel, with an unexpectedly sympathetic smile. "It wouldn't be the first time."

To tell the truth, I would have rather liked to, but after thirty or so years, I was out of practice. The best I could produce was a heavy sigh.

Annabel put her hand on my shoulder. "Do yourself a favor, stop worrying about Dad, will you, Ape?"

"Easy for you to say," I answered.

"Since when have you cornered the market on filial affection? Come on, you're going to be late," she said, leading me to the door. "I love him as much as you do, you know."

"Probably more," I said, trailing behind her. "But how much would you love him if he couldn't pay the rent, couldn't pay the tuitions, couldn't pay the food bills"—words were now tumbling out of my mouth faster than I was tumbling down the stairs—"no more fancy restaurants, or vacations, no more Health and Racquet Club, not even a park permit for tennis . . . how much will* you love him when your little pals ask you what he does for a living and you have to say, 'Nothing. His wife and kids left him, he lives all alone in a burned-out section of the South Bronx, sitting around in his undershirt all day, drinking beer out of a can, watching game shows, and waiting for the phone to ring, which it won't.' How much will you love him then!"

"Wha-at?!" Annabel came to a dead stop on the stairs—I nearly crashed into her. "What kind of lurid X-rated scenario is that!" she said, turning around to face me.

"Anybody who blabs company business to Peggotty Horn is going to get fired, Annabel. It has to be."

---

* Please note change of tense in midstream of thought from *would* to *will*.

"But you don't even know what he said to Peggotty Horn."

"I can imagine, though," I said grimly.

"Imagine, imagine! That's the trouble with you. This whole thing is nothing but pure conjecture and gross hyperbole, which means—"

"I know what it means," I said irritably—one year at Yale, the girl was a walking thesaurus, "but seriously, Annabel, let's say your dad did get—"

"He's your dad, too."

"Yes, well, if Dad did get fired, how *would* you feel? Seriously."

"Seriously?" She was on the verge of answering when Terry Mallison, my counselor, appeared, breathless, at the foot of the stairs behind her.

"Ben Andrews, they're waiting for you in Outward Bound."

"In a minute," I said. "Go on, Annabel." Too late. She was already turning her back on me—literally and figuratively.

"*Now,* Ben," said Terry, "Captain Wilking wants you *now.* He sent me to get you, spit-spot, on the double."

"Terrific," I said. "What are you, his Punctual Flunky?"

Annabel tittered girlishly. Oh-ho! I thought to myself, what's going on here? I hadn't heard that sound since Boris Harris—with whom she was madly in love five years ago— kissed her in the front hall. I was eavesdropping in the front-hall closet. (No apology; she was only fourteen, don't forget, and any responsible parent—oh, never mind.)

"Hello, Terry," she said. "Remember me?"

"That can't be *you*, is it, Annabel?" said Terry, evidently knowing full well it could be and was.

"None other," she said with a second titter and a toss of her tawny mane.

"You two know each other?" I asked.

"From the orthodontist," said Annabel, without bothering to look at me.

"Astonishing what can happen in just two years," murmured Terry, sizing her up and down . . . and up—and suddenly, ZAP! there was eye contact between them that would burn a hole through your hand.

"Your teeth look wonderful," he ogled.

"Thank you," purred Annabel. "So do yours." They exchanged winsome, well-occluded smiles.

"I'm in my last year at Harvard. You?"

"Yale. Sophomore. It was a wild winter, I can't wait to relax." A flutter and a sigh.

"How about relaxing with me tonight after taps?" A wink and a half smile.

"How about getting me to Outward Bound before Wilking chews me up?" As long as I was stuck in the godawful place, the least I could do was try to make a go of it.

"In a minute," they said together.

"What happened to spit-spot on the double?" I inquired acidly.

The not-so-Punctual Flunky broke eye contact with the

Tawny Titterer just long enough to ask me what my hurry was, then turned to her again.

"There's a place called Lookout Point you can row to on the other side of the lake where you catch a great view of the open sky. Shall we?"

"Sounds good, Terry, but I'm not off until Monday. . . ."

On and on and on they went, with the winks, and the titters, and the burbles, and the flutters, and the ogles, and the gurgles and the murmurs and the sighs—let me tell you, I could have dropped dead without their noticing!

I'll tell you something else: In the end, I found my own way to Outward Bound; it was plenty rough. But being a possessive father incarcerated in the body of his twelve-year-old son, unable to prevent an assignation between his nineteen-year-old daughter and her slimy, sleazy new boyfriend, is a whole lot rougher, I promise you.

Nine

The first spoonful of Frosted Flakes was on the way to my mouth when I was struck by an overwhelming urge to add a bunch more sugar to the bowl—making up, I guess, for all Mom's breakfasts of shredded beaver-board which she calls fiber and good for you.

I had no sooner satisfied the urge when another one struck. This urge, equally overwhelming but a lot harder to account for, was to turn on the *Today* show.

Why? I wondered. Why do I want to do that? I never do at home. The only person who ever watches the *Today* show at home is— Oh, NO, I remember something! . . . No, wait, maybe I dreamed it, please, *please*, I dreamed the whole phone call and Peggotty Horn is just some fat nobody from nowhere I'll never see again in my life. . . .

Until I turned on the *Today* show and there she was, running off at the mouth for five agonizing minutes about people and projects I'd never heard of; but then winding up with "And for those of you dying to know the inside scoop on that Galaxy takeover, one of the execs 'way up there' in the company told me confidentially last night that ex-Prez Ty Donovan, who insisted to this reporter he was *voluntarily* ankling to Indie Prod, was definitely axed. I also learned that his replacement, beauteous Stephanie Marshak, filmland's first female studio head, is known around Galaxy as the Killer Cream Puff. Beauty is as beauty does, Stephanie!"

So that was that. It was all over. Unless—a ray of hope—unless there are so many high-level execs at Galaxy, they won't know who to pin it on. . . .

The phone must've rung five or six times before I was aware of it, then three or four more times before I screwed up the courage to answer it.

"Hello," I finally whispered into the mouthpiece.

"Is this the Galaxy exec who's 'way up there'?" asked a male voice.

"Not any longer, obviously." Oh Dad, I'm so sorry! "Boy, you're mighty swift with the executions around here, aren't you? Ready, aim, fired before a guy's even finished breakfast." A bitter afterthought. "Who needs breakfast?" I pushed the tray away.

"Hold on, Andrews. How can I fire you, I just got fired myself—according to you," he added pointedly.

It was "axed" Ty Donovan; axed and angry.

"Ty, I never said that. Peggotty Horn put words in my mouth."

"Funny, it's usually the other way around," he said

wryly. "Aah, what's the difference, nobody ever believes that myth about independent production anyway. All I can say to you, fella, is you've got more guts than I thought. Just as well—after this morning, you're going to need them. Killer Cream Puff, my eye!" He ha-ha-ed mirthlessly and hung up.

So Indie Prod meant independent production. That was one mystery solved. But what did "you've got more guts than I thought" mean? If anybody had guts it was Dad—oh Jeeze Louise, the phone again. Was *this* the firing squad?

No, this was only the message operator to say while I'd been talking, Mavis Ohler had called to remind me about the Galaxy story meeting at ten o'clock in Mr. Weller's office.

What time was it now? I asked her. Eight-fifty-nine. And how long did it take from here to there? Beverly Hills to Burbank this time of day, I should allow a good forty minutes, she told me. I told her to order me a cab, please, I'd be down in fifteen.

Which I was. Unshowered but otherwise presentable—in tie and jacket, with teeth brushed, beard brushed, mustache brushed, *loafers* brushed, and I even remembered the briefcase.

But they hadn't ordered the cab.

"Why not?" I said to the doorman. "I asked for one."

"We assumed you'd forgotten about the pre-arranged rental, Mr. Andrews, and the operator had no way of knowing about it. That's Our Department."

With a proud flourish, he opened the door of a spanking-new Ford sedan. "The keys are on the dashboard, sir. Have a nice day."

It was very tempting. In fact, I was halfway in and about to ask the way to Burbank when a hysterical voice from the past screamed, "Don't ever get behind the wheel of a car. I want your solemn word on that! Do I have your solemn word?"

Did he or didn't he? I couldn't recall, but if he did . . .

Old Yellow Jell-O stepped back out.

"Anything the matter, sir?"

"Is this what my secretary requested? I'm sure I told her a Mercedes," I said, perplexed. (Well, I had to make up *some*thing, didn't I?)

"Oh, sir, I'm terribly sorry," said the doorman, hailing me a cab.

"Perfectly all right, I just don't want to be late for my ten-o'clock meeting," I said graciously, tipping him a dollar and climbing in.

"You won't be, sir. Get Mr. Andrews to Galaxy in Burbank before ten, will you, good buddy?" he said to the driver.

"No problem," said the driver.

He went like a bat out of hell and got me there at one minute of, so by the time I found Mr. Weller's office, I was still only five minutes late. Not that it mattered.

I could have missed the whole thing, for all they cared.

"Morning," I said cheerily, and to Tony Crane, the one person I recognized from having come for dinner once in New York, "Hi, Tony."

They—a couple of youngish women in slacks and, including Tony, four men about Dad's age wearing open shirts—looked up from the blue papers they were all studying and studied me instead. Briefly, but long enough to see something they didn't like. My clothes, I hoped.

"I haven't unpacked yet," I explained, loosening my tie and removing my blazer.

"Really? We heard you came in last night on the five," said toneless Tony. Without so much as a "have a seat, Bill," he and the others went back to their blue papers. The problem was clearly deeper than clothes.

Have you ever been to a shunning? A Puritan shunning where nobody talks to the sinner or takes notice of anything he does—even when he opens his briefcase upside down, nervously looking for his own blue papers—and one *Lampoon*, two *Penthouses*, and a pink hippo fall out on the floor? No? You haven't lived.

In the anteroom after the meeting, I made a final stab at détente. "Anyone for lunch?"

Coincidentally enough, every single one of them had other plans. Even I did, according to Mavis Ohler, Mr. Weller's secretary.

"Mr. Andrews, don't forget lunch in the commissary with Ray Ewald."

"Good old Ray Ewald!" Another friend of Dad's I'd met in New York; it was nice to know there was at least one person, other than Mavis Ohler, willing to communicate with me.

"And your appointment with Miss Marshak is at two," said Mavis, "but I guess you don't need reminding about that, do you." She sucked in her breath, crossed both sets of fingers on both hands, and added in a whisper, "Oh, gosh, good luck, we're all praying for you!"

Mavis Ohler may have looked like a prune in a polyester pants suit, but she was rapidly becoming my best friend.

"Thanks. Thanks a lot," I said gratefully, and kissed her good-bye on the cheek.

Finding the commissary—which I did by simply following a horde of people all headed for the same stucco building (at 1:00, where else would they be going?)—was easier than finding Ray Ewald. I checked the entire room, table by table, and the cafeteria line; he was nowhere to be seen.

To be seen were:

four Roman gladiators in breastplates and plumed helmets

a bevy of identically costumed show girls from one of

those 40's movies (good-looking girls)

an enormous fat man, a bearded lady (real beard, I think), three clowns, and two midgets, all eating at the same table, the midgets sitting on those baby seats that fit on regular chairs—must be a circus movie

three surgeons in green coveralls, an operating-room nurse, and a lady bandaged from top to toe, one arm in a cast—a hospital movie

some grease-streaked G.I.'s in camouflage jumpsuits

one werewolf

a seven-foot gorilla taking off his head in order to eat a fruit-salad platter brought to him by his five-and-a-half-foot gorilla girl friend (I guess it was a girl—she had a dainty way of walking)

some regular people in work clothes (unless they were actors in a movie about regular people who worked)

and me, who was too hungry to wait any longer for Ray Ewald—word travels fast out here; by now he was probably captain of the shunning team.

The bandaged lady, just behind me in the cafeteria line, needed help with her tray, so I carried hers and mine to a big table where, among G.I.'s, Romans, and show girls, I'd spotted two empty places.

"Here we go," I said, unloading tuna fish and chocolate milk for me, conch chowder and rice pudding for her—blech!

"How can you eat that stuff!"

She pointed to her wired jaw, and rolled her eyes. "No choice."

Boy, if that's what you go through being an actor, it's not worth it.

"How long is that thing on for?" I asked sympathetically.

She put up ten fingers.

"Ten days?"

With her hands, she indicated longer.

"Ten *weeks*?" Ten weeks, she must be the star of the picture. That might be worth it.

"What are you in?"

"What am *I* in?" she croaked. "A lot of pain. From a car accident." She shook her head in amazement. "It never occurs to you people there are other professions in this world besides acting, does it?"

For someone in a lot of pain, she was remarkably chatty, I thought.

"Sorry, it was dumb of me," I said.

"All actors are dumb," she announced. "What are you in, a remake of *The Man in the Gray Flannel Suit*?"

"This is the way we dress on the East Coast," I said aloofly.

One of the Romans picked up his ears. "I hear there's some East Coast Galaxy dude got canned this morning by the Killer Cream Puff herself."

"Says who?" My beard was standing on end.

"Says everyone. It's all over the lot."

Astonishing! Eight-thirty this morning Peggotty Horn goes on the air, by lunchtime the whole studio knows Marshak's nickname and my fate. Who needs lunch! Besides, it was almost two o'clock.

I pushed the tuna fish away and hastily excused myself from the table.

As I headed for the door, one of the show girls, referring to me, said, "What's he in?"

"Trouble, I think," said the Roman thoughtfully.

All actors are not dumb. . . .

I wonder how it's going to happen and how you're supposed to behave.

With dignity?: "Miss Marshak, I guess there's nothing I can possibly say—"

"I think you've said quite enough already, Mr. Andrews."

"Or do," I persist.

"Do?" She studies her blood-red talons for a moment, then smiles a Mona Lisa smile. "Yes, there is something you can do." Quick as lightning, a cruel forefinger points to the door. "Out!" she rasps. "Get out, now!"

With restrained outrage?: "Miss Marshak, firing me is your privilege, of course, but you might have done me the courtesy of informing me before you informed everybody else."

"*You* are accusing *me* of informing?! Ho-ho, that's rich!" A malevolent cackle, followed by "Out! Get out, now!"

She's got a point there. Scratch that one.

Unrestrained outrage?: "If you think I'm sorry I called you a Killer Cream Puff, you're right—it's too good a compliment for anyone as mean and horrible as you!"

No, too babyish.

Guile, maybe? "I never called you a Killer Cream Puff. It was Ty Donovan."

"Tainting your best friend with libel and slander, that's attractive, I must say!" she sneers. "Out!" she points. "Don't bother opening the door, just slither right under it, you contemptible worm!"

Scratch that one, too. I'm ashamed I even thought of it.

Candor. How about candor?: "Miss Marshak, if you fire me, you may well be destroying the career of an innocent man."

"Are you trying to tell me you did *not* discuss Galaxy affairs last night on the plane with Peggotty

Horn? Mr. Andrews, really!"

"No, I'm not, yes, I did, but my *dad didn't!*"

She leans forward, a flicker of interest in her beady little eyes. Now we're getting somewhere!

"I fail to see the connection . . ."

With relish, I connect her, beginning with the body exchange in the Port Authority terminal, ending with "So what you see before you, Miss Marshak, is only a twelve-year-old boy," here's where I start to cry, "who's very scared and homesick and Mom is in the desert with the Navajos," here's where I notice her blood-red talon pressing a button on the office intercom machine. "Hey, what are you doing that for?" and here's where she whispers into it, "This man is a hallucinating paranoid schizophrenic! I want you to call the little men in the white coats and tell them to get him out of here, *now!*"

"Okay, okay, I'll go," I moan, "but if Dad and I change bodies again while I'm in the cookie jar, will you give him his old job back?"

Tears are now cascading down my cheeks, my beard is sopping wet and dripping on my briefcase . . .

"Mr. Andrews?" What, *what,* who said that, where *am* I?! "Would you like a tissue, Mr. Andrews?"

Reality returned. I was in the waiting room of Stephanie Marshak's office. Waiting for my two-o'clock hour of judgment. Waiting, and crying—in front of Betty Lou Bienenstock, Stephanie Marshak's secretary.

I helped myself to several tissues, blew my nose, wiped my eyes, and blotted my beard.

"Rose fever," I explained.

"I understand," she said tactfully. "Look, this is none of my business, but whatever you do, don't do anything foolish."

"Like what?" What's left!

"Oh, like get on your high horse and say, 'You don't fire me, I quit!' or something like that."

"Sounds good to me. Why not?"

"Because you'll lose all your stock options and severance pay." She peered at me over the rims of her half glasses. "Forgive me for being personal—"

A buzzer sounded. Like a klaxon, it sounded. I jumped a foot.

"I'm afraid that's it, hon."

I rose, straightened my shoulders, strode manfully to the door—that was the easy part—and hesitated.

"Go on in," urged Betty Lou gently. "She's expecting you."

I opened the door.

Seated at the desk, head down, too engrossed in paperwork to acknowledge my presence, was the Killer Cream Puff. No red talons, I noticed. Just plain ordinary hands—but plenty capable-looking. Capable of signing a company death warrant, which was probably what she was doing right now. Aw, nuts, I might as well get it over with.

With my fingers, I beat a timid tattoo on the door-jamb.

She lifted her head. What I could see of her—the part that wasn't obscured by black aviator glasses—was, as Dad had described, devastatingly attractive on the surface—blond hair (natural), good nose, great mouth, but the coldest fish in filmdom underneath, I reminded myself.

"I don't quit, you fire me," I declared resolutely.

At that, she whipped off her aviator glasses and I nearly fainted dead away—partly from lack of breakfast and lunch, but mostly from shock.

Because gazing at me with those enormous deep-blue eyes of hers was my own beloved Miss Moon.

Ten

Wouldn't you know it, Hitzigger snores. And when Hitzigger snores, the whole tent shakes, including—especially including—the double-decker bunk he and I share. (For bed assignment the cabin drew lots. I drew Hitzigger; shot with luck, I am.)

Some people sleep through Hitzigger; I am not one of them, and between Thursday and tonight (Monday), I'd had approximately eight fitful hours of shut-eye—hardly enough for a growing boy. I could just see Ape Face at twenty, still only 4'11". ("Hey, shorty, what's the matter with you you're so short?" "It's called Hitzigger's Syndrome.")

Oh well, I grew to 6'1" myself; Ape Face should be genetically programmed to follow suit. . . . He'd better do it, too! I sat bolt upright in bed—adolescence was bad enough the first time, if I had to go through it twice . . . Crikey, Hitzigger, shut up! I pounded the sagging bedsprings under his butt.

We will now have a minute of silence in which to pray for ten more. Nothing doing; Mount Vesuvius is at it again.

From my neighboring bottom bunk, I enviously watched

the serene rise and fall of Duck's chest and hissed what I thought was a rhetorical question at him.

"How can you sleep through that!"

"What?"

I repeated the question, louder this time.

"Ravel? I love it—it *puts* me to sleep. Here, have a try."

"Thank you," said Mallison, intercepting the transistor on its way from Duck to me.

We heard the click of the lock on Mallison's Confiscated Articles strongbox, then the creak of bedsprings as he lay back down again. And then I heard . . . ?

"Duck," I whispered, "are you crying?!"

He answered with a couple of snuffles and a sniff.

"Aw, come on, Duck, you'll get it back at the end of the summer."

"I can't get *through* the summer without music, you know that."

"Aren't you two asleep yet? One more squawk and I'll have to give you each a demerit," warned Mallison.

After five minutes of relative silence (Hitzigger notwithstanding), Mallison creaked to a sitting position and checked the cabin for signs of life. Finding none, he quickly dressed himself and crept stealthily out of the cabin.

"Where's he going? He's supposed to be on duty," said Duck.

"To meet my daugh-um-sister at Lookout Point, the slimy sleaze bag. Some nerve he's got cracking down on us when he's breaking rules himself!"

No response.

"Are you asleep?" I asked.

"Of course not. I've just been thinking. About rules. I've read the rule book: three demerits equals one black mark; three black marks and they send you home. Well, if they hand out demerits for talking after taps, we could get ourselves kicked out of here in no time—I mean a demerit for talking, think what we'd get for swearing—"

"—or fighting. I could punch out Hitzigger!"

"That's no good. You'd lose and I wouldn't get a demerit. How about we both punch out Hitzigger?"

"You're on. How about we both streak in Sunday church service—hand in hand." I was beginning to enjoy this.

So was he. "Duck Levine and the panty-hose queen, together again!" he giggled. "But that's almost a whole week away, though. I don't want to wait that long, do you?"

"I *can't* wait that long," I said, thinking of Ape Face and Stephanie Marshak. "But you know something?" A brilliant idea had just popped into my head. "We don't have to. Listen, you know those enormous music books you keep under the bed?"

"My orchestral scores—what about them?"

"Grab a couple of really fat ones and get dressed. We're leaving now!"

Not until all the cabins and the admin building were safely behind us, and the road to freedom lay a few tantalizing feet ahead, did we finally stop to catch our breath.

"Ape, this is crazy," panted Duck. "We'll never make it—especially lugging nine Beethoven symphonies. What do we need them for?"

"You'll see."

"But yesterday we barely made it around the lake, and Moosehead Village is a ten-mile hike from here."

"Who said anything about hike? Pipe down and follow me."

I led him to a bunch of outbuildings where the camp van, a green Chevy number known as the Reluctant Dragon, was parked under an open shed.

I opened the door on the driver's side and climbed in. As anticipated, due to Hitzigger's Syndrome, I had an unobstructed view of the steering wheel.

"The Beethovens, please," I commanded.

Speechless, Duck passed them over and I slipped them under. A vast improvement, I thought smugly. I'm wonderful, I think of everything!

I leaned over and opened the door on the passenger side. "Hop in."

He hesitated.

"What are you waiting for—Mallison to chauffeur us to town personally? Hop in and close the door quietly."

He did. "But—" he began.

"Don't worry, I know how. I've known how for years. Now let's see"—I felt over the sun visor—"keys, keys, if you were the keys, where would you be?"

"Under Wilking's pillow," said Duck.

"You're a natural-born pessimist," I said, locating them under the rubber floor mat. "All righty"—I turned on the ignition—"one, two, three, and away we go!"

"Lights!" he howled. "You forgot lights!"

"Duck, old sock," I said, nose to the windshield, "you can either have lights and get caught, or no lights—"

"—and get killed."

"Nonsense, I know these roads like the back of my hand."

"Then how come you're going in the wrong direction? The front gate's back there."

"So is Wilking's house. The back way is up here. Or used to be."

And still was, I noted with satisfaction.

"See?" I crowed triumphantly as I made a left onto Route 42. "Now do you believe me?"

"So far so good," he conceded. "What I want to know is, how did you know—about the back way?" I'm not the only one who thinks of everything.

"Oh," I said, ad-libbing airily, "Dad described it to me."

I was getting pretty good at this dissembling game. In fact, instead of spending endless days in a South Bronx tenement with beer and television, I could probably be circling the globe as a double agent—assuming I repossess myself sometime in the near future. If not, a twelve-year-old double agent would be even more effective—who'd suspect him? Ape Face could spend *his* days in the Bronx tenement, serves him right for not springing me from camp when I told him to. . . .

Duck interrupted my reverie with "What's that big black thing up ahead?"

"Where?"

"In the middle of the road."

I swerved, not a minute too soon. "Wow, that's what I'd call a near moose!" Heh-heh.

"Very funny," said Duck, unamused. "I hope it's our last."

"You never can tell. They don't call it Moosehead Village for nothing, I imagine."

"Yeah, well, a moose head on a wall is one thing. A live head attached to a big black body is something else entirely," he complained.

"Grumble, grumble, grumble," I chided, making a right onto the main drag.

"Now where are we?" asked Duck.

"I 95, heading south."

"What'll we do when we run out of gas? We're pretty low now."

"Hitch."

"What if we get picked up by the cops?"

"We'll tell them we ran away from home but now we're sorry, so would they please deliver us back to our parents in New York."

"And if they know that's not true because Soonawissa-kit's already put out an alarm?"

"Then they'll take us back to Soonawissakit, where we'll get kicked out for running away from there, and the camp will have to deliver us to our parents in New York. Heads we win, tails they lose. Any other questions?"

"Not a one, Ape, not a one," he said, admiring me greatly, as well he might.

"Fine. Now it's my turn." I patted the CB radio resting on the transmission hump between the two front seats. "Do you know how to use one of these things?"

"Sure. The family I stayed with last summer when I was singing with the Santa Fe Opera had one."

"See what you can find out about the cop situation on this road, will you? I don't mind being picked up for hitchhiking, but being remanded to some New York State correctional home for juvenile car thieves, dope fiends, and switchblade murderers doesn't hold quite the same appeal, as I'm sure you'll agree."

"Gotcha," said Duck, turning on the CB.

The ensuing exchange between The Squeaky Bird[1] and B.B.[2], in our four-wheeler[3], and Tough Tiddly[4] and the Jolly Green Grape[4], running shotgun[5], on a bounce around[6] to

---

[1] Duck's CB handle, i.e., code name
[2] my handle. Stands for Big Bill, the best I could come up with on such short notice
[3] just what it sounds like
[4] I never found out their real names. Tough Tiddly was the driver
[5] driving partner
[6] return trip

Nastyville[7] in their eighteen-legged pogo stick[8], ought to win the Gobbledygook Award of the Year:

The bears[9] were crawling on the big slab[10] (no City Kittys[11], Duck was relieved to learn), and one in the grass[12] at Exit 12.

"So unless you're hankering for a Christmas card[13], better hammer off[14], Squeaky Bird," said Tough Tiddly.

Duck translated. I slowed to a legit double nickel[15] and instructed him to find out if there was a more indirect route to New York than I 95.

"What for an indirect route[16] to the Dirty Side[17], good buddy, you a skip shooter[18] or something?"

"10-4," affirmed Duck. "Plus we're almost out of motion lotion[19], entirely out of green stamps[20], we got a coupla slick

---

[7] Nashville

[8] eighteen-wheel tractor-trailer truck

[9] police switching from side to side of the expressway

[10] the expressway

[11] local police

[12] the median

[13] speeding ticket

[14] slow down

[15] I bet you can figure it out for yourself; I did. No? 55 M.P.H.

[16] there is apparently no code word for this—truckers don't use indirect routes

[17] New York City

[18] unlicensed CB user

[19] gas—true, too; the gauge read empty

[20] money—also true

tennis shoes[21], and lastly, me and B.B., running shotgun, are checkin' our eyes for pinholes[22]."

"That's real bad, Squeaky Bird," commiserated Tough Tiddly.

I took over the mike. "Tough Tiddly, B.B., here. If you're heading for the Dirty Side yourself by any chance, we sure would appreciate a lift, good buddy."

"Good thinking!" said Duck.

Tough Tiddly's reaction seemed encouraging. "How's about peeling off the slab at Exit 13 onto Route 201, hang a first right for Marty's Roadhouse, seven miles down the road, we can eyeball[23] it over some Kool-Aid."

"Fine, but nix the Kool-Aid," I told Duck. "I haven't had that stuff since I was a kid—a *small* kid—and I hated it then."

"Kool-Aid is liquor," explained Duck. "You'd hate that more[24]. Negatory on the Kool-Aid, Tough Tiddly."

"Coffee, coffee!" I prompted.

"—But a cup of mud would go down real good."

By them, this proposition (I use the word advisedly, as you'll soon see) was a definite 10-4—until they swaggered into Marty's and discovered its sole occupants, other than the bartender, were not what they'd been mistakenly led to expect.

---

[21] tire trouble—untrue

[22] tire*d* trouble—untrue, but sounded good

[23] meet

[24] that's what he thinks

"Muskrats![25]" Tough Tiddly was disgusted.

"*Male* muskrats!" The Jolly Green Grape was even more so.

"You thought we were seat covers[26]?!" gasped Duck.

"With girlie voices and handles like Squeaky Bird and Bibi, what else would we think?" growled Tough Tiddly.

"Gosh *darn!*" I exclaimed, smacking the tabletop. "That never occurred to me."

(It probably should have, too, but when all your energy is going into acting like a twelve-year-old boy, it really never crosses your mind you might be taken for a seat cover.)

"Me either," said Duck, sheepishly.

"Well . . ." said the Jolly Green Grape with a look at Tough Tiddly.

"Yeah, well . . ." he agreed.

"Well what?" asked Duck, a bundle of nerves.

"Whaddya mean, what? What what? Adios is what," said the not-so-Jolly Green Grape. He turned to leave; Tough Tiddly did the same.

Duck darted in front of them and I did the same. Between us, we blocked their access to the door.

"But what about our lift to the Dirty Side?" pleaded Duck.

"Yes, you see, we ran away from home but now we're

_____

[25] children
[26] attractive girls

90

sorry, so we were hoping you could help us get back," I added.

Tough Tiddly said, "Let's get something straight. You muskrats're running away *from* the Dirty Side or *to* the Dirty Side?"

"From," said I. "To" said Duck, both of us answering at once.

The Jolly Green Grape's response to this was either a stifled laugh or a belch—I couldn't tell which.

"What I mean is," I explained, "we *were* running away from there, now we're running *to* there."

"Then what's that four-wheeler with a Maine license plate doing parked out front?" asked Tough Tiddly.

Again, Duck and I both answered at once. "Um . . ."

"Uh-huh," said Tough Tiddly.

"Like I said before, adios," said the J.G.G.

Together, with humiliating ease, they broke through our pitiful phalanx and swaggered out. With sinking hearts, we heard the roar of the motor as they drove off in a huff.[27]

"What do we do now?" asked Duck, turning to me for help. As usual, and I wish he wouldn't because I take it all back. I do not think of everything. In fact, at this particular juncture—stranded as we were in a deserted roadhouse, seven miles from the nearest expressway entrance, almost

---

[27] an eighteen-legged pogo stick with two disgruntled truckers in it. Only kidding

out of motion lotion and completely out of green stamps—
I couldn't think of anything we could do except call camp and
ask them to come and get us.

Which is what we did, and I assure you, they were not
pleased.

Eleven

"Fire you? Why should I do that?"

"So I can get my stock options and severance pay."

"Ah"—she laughed—"but suppose I don't want to fire you?"

"Well, I'm not quitting, that's for sure," I said, plunking myself on the couch. I was wobbly in the legs.

"Good. That's all settled then." She seemed relieved. "Let's get down to business."

What are you doing here? Is it really you? Yes, it is, just thinner, that's all, how did you get here—from Miss Moon the teacher to Stephanie . . . was that your first name, Stephanie? I never knew . . . Marshak, head of Galaxy? . . .

Her lips were moving but it was like watching television with the sound off. I only tuned in for the tail end.

". . . story meeting?"

"Uh, sorry, what did you say?" I asked.

"I said how did the story meeting go?"

"Fine thanks."

Why doesn't she recognize me? Oh. Because she never really met Dad—only once in the second grade, without a beard, and not at all in the third grade, too busy at the ad agency.

So if she never met him/me, that means I can't tell her I'm not just any old Mr. Andrews, I'm *the* Mr. Andrews who's Ben's father, because with a new name and a new job, how would I know she used to be Miss Moon Ben's teacher since I never really met her I couldn't know that I think I'm going in circles.

". . . trip out?" I heard, tuning in again.

"Fine thanks, and you?" I answered. Do I dare tell her who I really am? No, no, no—remember the little men! Pay attention, jerk!

". . . a trifle distracted today, aren't you, Mr. Andrews? I didn't go anywhere, you did. I was asking about your trip out—which seems to have been rather"—she raised her eyebrows—"eventful."

I sighed. "Miss Marshak, I guess there's nothing I can possibly say—"

"No-oo," she interrupted, "but there's something I'd like to say."

Here it finally comes. What took her so long?

"What," I said, knowing full well.

"Thank you," she said.

"What?" I couldn't believe my ears. She must be kidding, but she was smiling.

"Which word didn't you understand?"

It was Miss Moon of the good old days—funny, friendly, teasing. ("Ben Andrews, yours was the highest score in the spelling test, so you get to pass the juice and cookies." "Who, me?" "Which word didn't you understand?")

"Look, Mr. Andrews—or Bill, if I may, may I?"

Vigorously, I nodded yes.

"Stephanie," she said, tapping herself. "Look Bill, when you told Peggotty Horn I was a Killer Cream Puff—did you make that up, by the way? It's perfect—"

"You're not like that, I'm sure you're not, I *know* you're not!"

"No"—she appreciated the compliment, I could tell by her eyes—"but to make it in this job, I should be. Now, thanks to you, everybody thinks I am and will treat me accordingly—with a great deal of respect that I'm actually not entitled to at all."

She threw back her head and laughed. "If you knew what I was doing only five years ago, you'd never believe it."

It was irresistible. "Teaching?"

"Yes, teaching!" If I'd guessed her zodiac sign she couldn't have been more delighted. "That's incredible!—Or did Ty tell you?"

"Nuh-uh," I said modestly.

"Well, either I have Teacher written all over me or you're positively clairvoyant."

Happily, she recalled her past. "Yep, five years ago, I was teaching second and third graders in New York, and if I went to a movie more than once a month it was because someone else took me—I certainly couldn't afford it."

"Then what happened?"

"Then I married one of those someone elses—not a very nice one, I'm afraid"—she smiled ruefully—"and we moved to California, where he got a top job at Boeing Aircraft and I got a divorce."

Whew, that's good. Not that I could marry her anyway, I'm already married . . . to my MOTHER! Ye gods, I don't want to be married to my mother, I don't care what Freud says. I mean, I love her a lot, but I don't want to be married to her and I'm sure she won't want to be married to me either when she knows who I am, but if I tell her, here we go again with the little men in the white coats—

". . . boring the pants off you, I'm afraid," said Miss Moon.

"No! No, no, it's fascinating, go on, please, please go on," I begged her. Later, I'll worry about my wife later.

"Well," she said, "after the year teaching kid actors on location, I'd picked up enough to get myself hired as a script girl at Magno-International, and from there I wormed my way into the story department at Paragon, then they made me head of the story department at

Paragon, and after that I went over to T.S.G. as Vice President in Charge of Production, and well—miracle of miracles, here I am."

"Just like that." I snapped my fingers.

"Just like that—oh, you know how it is," she said diffidently, "they have a funny way of doing things out here."

"So I've noticed," I said.

We both laughed, then there was an awkward silence, broken by her.

"Bill"—something about her voice made me suspect the Official Meeting had begun—"my spies tell me you have a wife and two children, that you're very ambitious," I am? "also very charming," that's nice, "and extremely good at your job." That's even nicer.

"So far, I can only attest to the charm element"—she grinned, I grinned back—"but assuming the rest of the information is accurate, how would you like to move your family and your charming ambitious self out here where you can be extremely good at an even better job—specifically, Vice President in Charge of Worldwide Production."

Pleased with her offering, she leaned back in her chair and concluded with "Oh, and you needn't feel you have to give me an immediate answer, Bill. Take all the time you want."

"Okay," I said.

There was another awkward silence.

"Naturally, you'll have all the concomitant increases and extras—that goes without saying," she added.

I waited.

Anxiously, now, she leaned forward in her chair. "Don't forget, the company will pay for the move, help you get a house, find schools for the kids, et cetera, et cetera—the lawyers will work out details later—if you're interested, that is, and I hope you are. I could use a fellow New Yorker."

"Which word didn't you understand?" Tit for tat, Miss Moon! "I already said okay."

"Oh!" she exhaled with relief; then, imitating me earlier, she snapped her fingers. "Just like that? You can make up your mind just like that?"

Wouldn't Dad? Of course he would. Besides, he wasn't there to ask. I'd just have to stand on my own two feet and make up my own two minds.

"Just like that," I said.

"What about your wife?" Her again! "After all, relocating to the West Coast—that's rather a big step to take without consulting her, isn't it?"

"Not at all," I said. "We have an old-fashioned marriage—wherever I go, she goes."

A flicker of disapproval crossed her face. "You're very fortunate."

"Or"—I made a generous concession—"if she and the kids are really miserable about living here, they can stay put and I can commute back and forth in my spare time."

There, that would take care of the wife/mother problem! And Annabel wouldn't care where we lived, she was at Yale, anyway. As for Dad, I absolutely didn't need him hanging over my shoulder all the time, monitoring my every move. I'd gotten this far without him, I could go the whole distance . . . which could be . . . *forever,* come to think of it! I'm not so sure I'd like forever. . . .

". . . awfully happy about this, Bill," said Miss Moon, ushering me to the door.

"Oh, me, too," I said, opening it. "Just one favor, can I borrow a—no, *may* I borrow a phone?"

"Ah," she exclaimed, "you're a man after my own heart, Bill Andrews. Nobody speaks decent English anymore."

"A lot depends on the teacher," I told her, "and mine was terrific."

Twelve

The next morning (Tuesday) at breakfast, Letty "Ma Barker" Newsome, the camp nurse, stopped by our table to tell Duck and me we were wanted upstairs in the admin office as soon as we'd finished eating.

Duck, having just closed his lips around a spoonful of dank mucilage (oatmeal), removed the spoon, contents intact, and slapped it back in the bowl.

"I'm finished now," he said jauntily.

"Likewise," I said, shoving my bowl into the middle of the table.

Snorkel Bains shoved it back to me again. "You two are finished when I say you're finished and not a minute before."

Thor Swensen noted the look of revulsion on my face. "The condemned man ate a hearty meal," he snickered.

"That's right, Ape," encouraged Duck, zealously tucking into his mucilage, "the sooner we eat, the sooner we get condemned."

"And the sooner you get condemned, the sooner we get

you two faggots out of my cabin, so eat up, Andrews," said Guess Who.

"Knock it off, Hitzigger," cautioned Bains.

"Yeah, Hitzigger, knock it off," said Woodruff Somebody-or-Other.

"Oh, that's okay," I said, scrupulously scraping minispecks from the bottom of my bowl, "we don't mind, do we, Duck."

"Not a bit," he said, winking at me.

I returned the wink, and rose from the table, as did he. And then, feature this, if you will, Duck Levine and the panty-hose queen, together again, walked the entire length of the dining room, hand in hand. What did we care—we were leaving anyway!

The problem was, we weren't.

"Not that you don't deserve to be kicked out . . ." Wilking scowled at us from behind his desk; Annabel and Terry Mallison stood dutifully to one side. "And not that Soona-wissakit wouldn't be well rid a ya . . ." He scraped viciously at the inside of his pipe, then emptied it into a glass ashtray. "But Sis, here, tells me yer momma's gallavantin' around in the desert somewheres, unreachable by any means, be they telephone, telegraph, carrier pigeon, or Pony Express, and yer poppa's much too busy gettin' rich 'n' famous to take charge a ya hisself—"

"That's nonsense," I said.

"No, it's not," said Annabel, looking very cat-that-swallowed-the-canary-ish. "Read this."

She stuck a Mailgram under my nose:

HAVE ACCEPTED GALAXY PROMOTION
TO VICE PRESIDENT OF WORLDWIDE
PRODUCTION. DETAILED LETTER FOL-
LOWS. LOVE AND KISSES, SUPERDAD.

"Ohmigod, ohmigod, that's incredible!" I babbled.

"Watch that mouth!" thundered Wilking.

"Sorry, sir, sorry, sorry, sorry, a million pardons! Annabel, that is stupendously good news!"

"Fer yer poppa it is," said Wilking. "Fer us, it means we got no choice but to keep you here all summer. . . . Sh . . . oot!" He thwacked his pipe on the ashtray, cracking the ashtray and shearing the pipestem neatly in two.

"Aw, Ape, aw gee, Ape!" said Duck, devastated in my behalf.

"It's okay, Duck," I said bravely. "Now that I know Dad's all right, I don't mind staying." Until Ape's letter arrives and I can see what's what.

"As for Captain Wilking . . ." My eyes did a slow, disdainful crawl from the broken pipestem to his glowering, sour puss. "Well, sir, if I can put up with you, I guess you can somehow manage to put up with—"

"*Both* of you!" Wilking said angrily. "Not just one, but—"

"Both!" squealed Duck. "Why both? My parents aren't too busy to take me. I mean, they're busy, but not that busy. I can make myself very useful—typing Mom's book, assisting Dad—"

Annabel exploded with laughter. "In neurosurgery? His father's a neurosurgeon," she explained to Mallison and Wilking.

"In the office, stupid, in the office," shouted Duck, purple in the face. "Or I'll read the *Encyclopedia Britannica,* or sing in the street for small change, I'll do anything, for crumb sake, but you have to kick me out, *please!*"

"Be reasonable, Arthur," urged Mallison. Arthur? Funny, he doesn't look like an Arthur. "We can't kick out one of you and not the other."

"That's the stupidest thing I ever heard—we're not joined at the hip!" said Duck.

"Just at the hands," snorted Wilking. "Forty years a Soonawissakit, we never had a pair a sissies like you!"

"Right!" I chimed in. "So split us up."

"Just what we ought to do, Captain," said Mallison. "Andrews can stay in Mount Olympus and we can transfer Levine to High Ledge."

"No, no, no!" protested Duck. "I want to be kicked out. Come on, kick me out!"

"Oh, Arthur, look," said Mallison. "It's very simple. As I understood the facts from Ben last night on the phone, it was he who masterminded the whole hare-brained scheme, and he who drove the van—"

"Yes, but he doesn't get all the credit. I'm the one who used the CB radio. Illegally! I'm just as much a criminal as he is—every bit!"

"That may be," said Mallison doggedly, "but how would it

103

look to your parents if we expelled you and kept him? They'd have a perfect right to sue."

"We haven't had that happen in forty years, neither," said Wilking. "They're both stayin' and that's final."

Something told me—the resolute look on der Führer's face, probably—that we were flogging a dead horse. Duck, on the verge of tears, evidently thought so too. I decided to salvage what I could from the situation.

"I guess Mr. Mallison's right, Duck," I said slyly. "Your parents might also sue for negligence—since it was insufficient supervision that led to the transgression in the first place."

"Wordy little kid, aren'tcha," said Wilking. He turned to Mallison. "What's he talkin' about—insufficient supervision? I thought you were asleep when they left."

"Well, actually . . ." I looked pointedly at Annabel and Mallison; mutely but eloquently they beseeched me to shut up. "Actually, I suppose being a heavy sleeper isn't exactly negligent . . ."

"Durn tootin' it's not," said Wilking, much relieved. But not as relieved as Annabel and Mallison.

To sum up the rest of the conversation, Mallison responded to my blackmail maneuver by suggesting that it wouldn't really be necessary to put Duck and me in separate cabins as long as he kept a careful eye on us. Wilking, after grumbling that one eye wasn't good enough, finally agreed—but warned us he didn't want any more of that sissy stuff, we should save it for Greenwich Village. Then it was case dismissed, and

Mallison told us we were free to rejoin our friends in the scheduled morning activities.

"Friends? What friends?" groused Duck as we were macho-marching to the table we had optimistically vacated only ten minutes before. The hostility in that completely silent dining room was so thick you could choke on it.

"I think it's time we made some," I told him.

A lone, lewd whistle pierced the chilly still; within seconds, it had triggered a scene reminiscent of the one on the bus, but worse by a country mile. No mere aisleful, now, but an entire roomful of loathsomely like-minded little boys undulated and lisped through a full chorus of "Yeth, Thir, That'th My Baby" while Duck and I tried to shoulder our way to our seats.

"Who'd want us? How're we going to do it?" shouted Duck over the din.

"I don't know," I answered, "but it's got to be done, and soon!"

The time to act was now.

"Duck, where's Hitzigger?" I yelled.

Duck's eyes nearly popped out of his head.

"A hundred and fifty kids in this camp, and you want *Hitzigger* for a friend? You're insane!"

"I don't want him for a friend, I want him for an enemy. Where is he? Just lemme at him!" I snarled, starting off to find him.

Duck grabbed me by the shirt and hauled me back. "You've already *got* him for an enemy."

"Not a public enemy," I said, shaking myself loose, "and cut that out, I can take care of myself."

"But you're only going to get creamed!" howled Duck.

He was right, of course, and getting creamed wasn't exactly my idea of a fun Tuesday, but if by making a public enemy out of Hitzigger, I could make a public hero out of myself, it was well worth it, under the circs.

"Ape, Hitzigger weighs a ton and fights mean. At least let's punch him out together like we planned," pleaded Duck.

I hesitated. Considering what I was stuck with in terms of external packaging, it was a tantalizing offer . . . but just then the kids launched into a second, even louder chorus of "Yeth, Thir," and I was more than ever determined to be the sole star of the creamation.

"Two against one is no way to make friends," I said, "and besides, from now on, it's every man for himself."

Duck cupped his hand behind his ear and leaned forward. "What?"

"Forget it," I shouted. Flexing a biceps and clenching a fist, I bellowed, "Where's Hitzigger? I wanna bust him one right in the chops! Hitz-ig-*ger?!*"

Suddenly it was as though there'd been a short circuit in the audio system—you could have heard a feather drop. Everyone stood stock-still, all eyes focused either on me or right behind me.

"Did I hear thomeone thay they wanted to butht me one?" asked Hitzigger, his voice a sinister combination of menacing and coy.

I froze in my tracks, clenched fist in midair. Hitzigger *behind* me I hadn't counted on!

"Here I am, thweetie," he taunted.

I could just picture him—hands on hips, simper on face, murderous, gay-baiting glint in eye . . . hands on hips, simper on face, murderous—oh, what the hell—

Quickly, I wheeled around . . . *and knocked him out cold on the floor!* It was easy—his hands were on his hips, he didn't have time to defend himself.

Chalk one up for our team!

Thirteen

Tues., July 5,

Dear Dad,

Hold it! Duck and I are always reading over each other's shoulders—there are no secrets between him and me—and if Duck reads Dear Dad over Dad's shoulder . . .

I sighed. This would have to be our first secret. I changed "Dad." Good thing I had an erasable pen.

Dear Ape Face,

How would Dad sound in a letter, what would he say first? . . . Got it!

> How's camp? Fine, I'll bet. That's good. I'm sure you're going to have just as much fun as I did when I was there.
> How's the weather been? Today it's 94° and sunny out here. I'm in my swimming trunks at the pool

aw, who did that?!

                                    as you can
        see by that splotchy place in the corner.

I'd brought only one piece of stationery out with me and was not about to make a marathon trek all the way back to my room for another one. There was probably stationery in the lobby, but since de Virgilio took such a dim view of improper attire in his precious lobby . . .

"I'm glad to see you here, Mr. Andrews."

Speak of the devil.

"No thanks to you, de V.," I said with a big grin to show I was only kidding.

I forgot; in Hollywood, funnyness is not the way to go.

"Please try to understand, sir, rules are rules" was his sober reply.

"Mm-hm" was mine. I started back to my letter.

"Mr. Andrews." De V. had something more to say. "Bob the Doorman wanted to have a word with you in the lobby."

"How's right now?" I asked, hooking my thumbs under my armpits and waggling my fingers at him.

He didn't take me seriously, but neither did he smile. "At your convenience, sir," he said with a business-like nod, then he clickety-clacked away in his shiny shoes.

I'm going to make that stiff laugh if it's the last thing I do!

Now, where was I?. . .

> I hope the news about my promotion put your mind at ease. I would've let you know sooner, but when I tried to phone you right after the meeting, all the circuits were busy, and then

I was having such a great time, it slipped my mind altogether until Monday when Mavis Ohler, who had been reassigned to me (all I had to do was request her and I got her—that's what I call power!), asked how Mrs. Andrews had taken my wonderful news.

I explained she hadn't heard it yet because there were no phones in the desert . . . phones!. . . Dad!— but my son Ben, at camp, would love to know; would Mavis take a Mailgram, I'd pay for it as soon as I could cash a check.

Oh, that wouldn't be necessary, laughed Mavis; for little things like that I was Galaxy's guest. Also, Galaxy would be glad to cash my check—if I'd make it out, she'd have the money for me by the end of the day.

Neat-o, I told her, and while she was up, could she buy (with my money) some transistor batteries and send them to my son's friend, Arthur Levine, same camp, same address as the one I was about to give her?

It would be her pleasure, said Mavis, and took care of the whole thing. Mavis is *terrific*!

Back to business . . . all the circuits were busy and then . . .

I was

completely tied up

doing Disneyland, surfing at Malibu, roller-skating in Venice (California), and going on every roller coaster at Magic Mountain with good old Ray Ewald (it turned out when I thought he was shunning me on Friday, he was waiting for me in the executive dining room—I didn't know there was one—thinking I was shunning *him*).

Ray's wife was also away on a trip, so he was delighted to fool around all weekend doing kid things with me because "I have the soul of a kid myself." That's an exact quote! I could hardly keep a straight face. Ray is terrific, too. (More about that later.)

Let's see, how does it sound so far . . . all the circuits were busy and then I was completely tied up . . . tied up with . . . tied up with what? Ah!

with a ton of paper-
work and business meetings—you know
how that is.

111

"There is a telephone call for Mr. Andrews, telephone for Mr. William W. Andrews," boomed the loudspeaker.

"Where?" I said out loud.

"By the bar, where it always is," said the guy in the next cabana.

I thanked him and managed to make it without mishap to the phone. (Not as easy as it sounds. Even at twelve noon on a weekday, the poolside is jammed at the Bev Hills; picking your way through a minefield of oiled, baked bodies requires the skill of a seasoned Marine.)

"Bill Andrews here," I announced into the phone.

"Oh, Mr. Andrews, honey"—it was Mavis—"the bank just called. You made the funniest mistake—you put your son's signature on that check instead of your own!"

Funny once, not so funny twice, you bozo!

That was because he was so much on my mind, I told her; I'd make out a new check tomorrow if the bank could wait that long. She assured me the bank could; then, after exhorting each other to have a nice day, we both hung up.

I returned to my terry-toweled chaise, ordered a liquorless piña colada, and began practicing William W. Andrews on the back of the poolside menu.

Midway through the nineteenth signature—which

was beginning to look quite legitimate—the loudspeaker announced a call for, of all people, Mr. Tyson Donovan.

Ty Donovan here? I took a furtive look around.

Yes, indeed, here: the guy in the next cabana who'd told me where the phone was (without even saying hello, Bill, how are you—he must be pretty mad; on the other hand, I didn't say hello to him either). He tossed aside his *Daily Variety*, jumped up, and sped to the phone.

When he reappeared, I exclaimed cordially, "Ty, I didn't recognize you!"

"I didn't expect you to," he said, settling himself back down with *Daily Variety*. "Now that I've been axed."

Zap.

"No, no, *no*, Ty, don't be silly! I didn't recognize you because—" quick, dummy, think of something! "—because you've lost so much weight—haven't you lost a lot of weight since the last time I saw you?"

Ty studied me carefully to see if I was bulling or not, and decided to believe me.

"Oh, about ten or twelve pounds, I guess." He put aside the *Daily Variety*—for good, I sensed. "Sorry about that, Bill," he said, referring apparently to the axed crack. "I'm suffering from a slight case of bruised feelings these days."

"Sure." I nodded to show I understood. "Listen, I'm sorry, too. About indie prod and stuff." Which I was. He seemed really nice.

"Yeah, well, it could be worse. Not that the phone's ringing off the hook yet or anything, but the money's okay for a while"—he knocked wood on the chaise—"and I've got a couple of genuinely exciting projects in the works."

The words were convincing, but the tone reminded me of Duck the day he told me he thought his voice was changing so fast he wouldn't be able to do the Metropolitan Opera broadcast but I shouldn't worry, it wasn't the end of the world—when I knew it temporarily was.

"That's good," I said, answering him the same way I'd answered Duck.

Changing the subject abruptly, Ty reached out and slapped me on the knee. "Son of a gun, I almost forgot—congratulations on the executive stripes!" He shook his head admiringly. "Gotta hand it to you, fella, you've got more guts than I thought."

That's the second time. Why does he keep saying that?

"What do you mean by that, Ty?"

"Oh, you know," he said vaguely.

"No, I don't, and I wish you'd tell me," I said.

Ty cleared his throat and shifted position uneasily. "Well, frankly Bill, in spite of a reputation to the contrary, you've always struck me as a sort of second banana."

Dad a second banana?! I must've looked startled.

"Plenty smart and personable, and *likable*," he added quickly, "but not the male equivalent of a Killer Cream Puff, and certainly not someone who'd dare call *her* one on national television. Whew!"

He wiped imaginary sweat off his brow. "That was a bold, aggressive move, Billy boy, and politically savvy, but it could have backfired. Yes, sir, a big, gutsy gamble that could've backfired and didn't—more power to you."

He paused for reflection, then said wonderingly, "I dunno, pal, I guess I just didn't realize you were capable of that kind of strategic one-upmanship."

"But I'm not!" I said, suddenly more worried about Ty's friendship than Dad's reputation. "It was all a weird accident. Believe me, when I talked to Peggotty Horn on the plane, I didn't even know who she was!"

"Bill, Bill," he said, raising a hand in protest, "spare me the lies, please! Look, it's all right. People do what they have to do. It's just that underneath the self-confident surface, I always figured you for a vulnerable type of guy—"

"But I am, Ty, I am! In fact, I'm so vulnerable I'm scared to death I'm going to get fired from this job before I start because, you know something? I'm in way over my head!"

Which was undoubtedly true and I just hadn't realized it until now.

"Well," said Ty quietly, "if that's really the case," and he finally seemed convinced I meant it, "I'd be careful who I admitted it to, if I were you. Actually, if I were you, I wouldn't even admit it to me."

What a crazy thing to say!

"Ty, that's ridiculous! If I can't trust you, who can I trust?—you're a good friend!"

And now for the zinger.

"No, I'm not," said Ty wearily. "I hate to disillusion you, sonny boy, but you don't have a good friend, and neither do I. Neither does anybody, not in *this* town."

He stood up, stretched, yawned, jammed his feet into his sandals, and said, "As for who you can trust, your wife is who, and be glad you have her. Mine walked out on me six months ago."

Having delivered this dour parting shot, he took off, leaving me with a whole bunch of thoughts that bugged me all day and half the night. Such as:

If you give the impression of being ambitious, aggressive, a strategic planner, in other words, a killer, it's as good as being one—better maybe, because you don't have to really *be* that way, you can remain a nice person who's just pretending. Like Miss Moon. Like Dad?

WHAT ABOUT DAD? Ty had him pegged as a second banana and acted disappointed and hurt when (thanks to Miss Moon's spies and my goof with Peggotty Horn) the company pegged him as a first banana and rewarded him accordingly. Is this because Ty is a deposed first banana himself, and jealous? I sort of don't think so—I stick by my first impression of Ty: a really nice guy . . . which would make him a second banana who got deposed—because he wasn't good enough at pretending? But if *this* is true, then Ty is disappointed in Dad because he thinks Dad was a first banana and a killer all along.

But was he, is he? Or is he just a terrifically successful pretender? When you come right down to it, what's the difference between the two? And who's to know which of the two you really are?

Only your wife, apparently, because according to Ty, you can't trust anyone else. Not even your kids, apparently, because why else would I be sitting in my Bev Hills hotel room at three in the morning asking myself *WHAT ABOUT DAD?*

More to the point, *WHAT ABOUT ME?* On a banana scale of 1 to 2 (first banana and second banana being all there is), I'd have to rate myself at least a 14 in one of my rare assertive moods, and somewhere in the high 30's otherwise. With a personality like that, how long can I go on fooling all of the people all of the time? Even more to the point, how long do I want to?

I can't think about this anymore.

FURTHER LATE-NIGHT REFLECTIONS ON OTHER SUBJECTS

On Identity

Being first in line for a hit movie gets you a good seat. Being first in line in the school lunchroom gets you a good choice of sandwiches. Being first in line at the Bev Hills Polo Lounge gets you nowhere, because the captain won't give you a table unless he knows who you are.

"Right this way, Mr. So-and-So." He beckons to some late arrival Big Shot in the back of the line.

"Malcolm, you're a brick," says the Big Shot as he shoots past the rest of us peasants.

"Wait a minute, Malcolm, I've been here for twenty minutes," you complain.

"How's a table for two in the patio?" he asks.

"Great," you say, stepping forward.

But he's not talking to you, he's talking through you (transparent Plexiglas, that's what you are!) to a Miss Big Shot who's been breathing down your neck from behind.

You step back in line again, she steps out and around you. A deep growl resonates in your cavernously empty stomach. There is a fierce ache in your salivary glands.

But now, ah-ha!, the phone on Malcolm's reservation desk rings. He answers it; he listens.

"Who?. . ." Bored, he scans the line. "I don't know. Never heard of him." He listens some more. "Oh . . . oh, really?" Impressed, he scans the line again. Then, setting the receiver down, inquires, "Is there a Mr. William Andrews here?"

Only since the day before yesterday, you turkey! would be a good answer. But you don't dare.

Instead, you settle for an understated raising of the hand and a subtle dig: "A Mr. William Andrews? How many of us are there?"

"*The* Mr. William Andrews, new Vice President of Galaxy, I should have said, sir," amends Malcolm with an unctuous smile.

He then goes on to say Bob the Doorman is most anxious to have a word with me (still! I forgot all about him). If I'd care to see him now, he'd have a lovely table in the patio waiting for me when I returned.

That's more like it!

On Power

Power is great for getting reservations, but when dealing with people like Bob the Doorman who's supposed to cater to the whims of people like me, better watch your step.

My whim (if you've forgotten, go back to Page 71)—a navy-blue Mercedes 480-SL convertible—was parked smack in front of the hotel where, according to a reproachful Bob, it had been waiting for me all morning. Did I intend to drive it today? Because otherwise he'd have the parking attendant take it away till tomorrow.

But what would I do with it then? This car problem was going to have to be solved once and for all.

"I don't intend to drive it ever," I told him. "Didn't my secretary mention that either? I want a chauffeur."

"A *chauffeur*, sir?" He seemed surprised. Which word didn't he understand?

"Yes, a chauffeur. Available at all times, night or day, beginning with four o'clock this afternoon. As you may have heard, I'm in the market for a house here, and I want to check out some of the better neighborhoods, so could you please get me someone who really knows his way around," because I don't. It's all I can do to find my room.

Well, folks, at four o'clock on the dot, a nine-hundred-year-old Englishman in a black suit and tie, white shirt, leather gloves, peaked cap—the works— was waiting for me in front of my Mercedes.

I drew Bob aside. "Is that my *driver*?"

"No, sir," corrected Bob, pleased as punch at having catered to another of my whims on such short notice. "That's your *chauffeur*. His name is Barkham."

(*Barkham*. Can you believe it—*Barkham?!*)

A piece of incidental intelligence: In Hollywood, if all you want is a plain, ordinary garden-variety driver who looks and acts like a regular person, don't ask for a chauffeur. A chauffeur is a driver with an idiotic name in an idiotic costume who makes you sit in the backseat—where you feel like a jerk—and is so stultifyingly boring and snobbish you fall asleep before you've seen even one third of Beverly Hills, let alone Brentwood, Westwood, Bel Air, or Pacific Palisades.

Conclusion: Power has its pitfalls.

More on HoJo's vs. the Bev Hills

I hate to keep harping on this, but in the food department, HoJo's wins again.

By the time I came back to my lovely table in the patio, I was so hungry I could've eaten the menu. Especially after I read it, because there was nothing on there I wanted to order.

"Couldn't I just have a peanut butter and jelly sandwich?" I asked the waiter.

"But of course, Mr. Andrews," he said, rushing off.

Ten minutes later, which even for HoJo's is the speed of light, he rushed back with a nine-dollar (!) Peanut Butter Platter: four dainty, crustless, toasted (I hate toasted, it's too runny) sandwich morsels surrounded—practically engulfed—by bushes of parsley, delicate carrot fronds and radish rosebuds. When I want a garden, I'll ask for a garden!

More on Identity

Meager as the edible part of my lunch was, I hardly had time to eat it, due to half the Polo Lounge coming up to say hello and congratulate me on the great Galaxy news. It must have spread like wildfire while I was out negotiating for Barkham, because nobody but Malcolm knew me when I left, and now everybody knew me but I didn't know them.

With one exception—Peggotty Horn. She kissed me on both cheeks, plunked herself down at the table, systematically defoliated my garden—which was okay with me—and had to be introduced to all those anonymous fans—which was not okay at all.

For a while, I got away with Dad's Old Trick: When he and I run into someone he can't think of the name of, he says, "You know my son Ben, don't you?" to which the person usually says, "Hi, Ben," and Dad never has to come up with the name. (The first time he worked that scam though, after saying, "You know my son Ben, don't you?" *I* said no, and since he couldn't come up with the name, the man went away insulted. Dad acknowledged it wasn't my fault but warned me the next time, for Pete's sake, to keep my mouth shut.)

Well, I was doing nicely with "You know Peggotty Horn, don't you?"—because most people actually did and vice versa, but then a big fat man came along and said no, he didn't.

"Well, here she is," I said with a feeble smile.

"Harvey Godchaux," he said, shaking her hand. To me he said testily, "Your lawyer, remember me? We spoke on the phone only this morning about ironing out the final kinks on your Galaxy deal?"

"Good Lord, Harvey, I didn't recognize you!" because you've *lost so much weight*! Pretty lame but it would have to do. "Haven't you lost a lot of weight lately?"

Godchaux sucked in his breath and gave his rotund tum a proud pat. "Nice of you to notice," he said. All was forgiven.

Henceforth, this weight-loss gambit shall be dubbed Ape's Old Trick. I used it frequently throughout my Hollywood stay and it never failed me.

One cautionary note, however. Don't use it in reverse—for example, "Millicent, I didn't recognize you, you've gained so much weight!" because Millicent will hate you forever, and if Millicent turns out to be Ray Ewald's wife just back from a health spa, you'll live to regret it. (More about that later.)

On Letter Writing
Don't try to finish a letter late at night when you're sleepy. Save it for later in the week when there's more to report anyway.

Fourteen

Tues., July 5th

Despite stunning victory over Hitzigger, was not carried out of dining room on shoulders of newfound admirers amidst cheers and huzzahs of exultant throng.

Instead, settled for dignified and Duck-less (my decision, not his) solo exit amidst discreet murmurs of praise and restrained back-pats from a scattered few. One triumph does not a hero make—this process would take time.

Volunteered for strenuous white-water canoe trip with de Menocal, Swensen, Biddle, Loring, and Hitzigger (!) with Snorkel Bains as leader. Duck didn't like the sound of it, elected not to come.

On short detour up Squangit River—which seemed vaguely familiar—Bains pointed out rope dangling from tree branch overhanging rushing river. Any takers? he challenged.

There were three possibilities: 1) Swing out far enough to dive safely into fathomless pool of glacially cold, clear water. 2) Swing out only far enough to dash yourself to

124

death on jagged rocks protruding from turbulent water directly below. 3) Sit humiliated and shivering on bank while everybody else played Tarzan and called you chicken—which Bains pointed out was what my dad had done 30 years ago. (He didn't have to tell me—I suddenly remembered it all too well.)

This time, I was first to take plunge (glacially cold is an understatement), winning respect of all, even Hitz.

Chalk *two* up for our team.

That night after supper, snuck out of Group Sing (a practice session of camp songs and cheers led by Annabel), helped Garland, Beaty hoist canoe paddles up flagpole. A sudden sneezing attack (mine) alerted Mallison, who threatened to report us. Wouldn't if I were you, I told him. P.S., he didn't. Garland, Beaty impressed.

Wed., July 6th
Tried out for cross-country team . . . qualifiers to compete Sat. in Southern Maine Intercamp Track Meet, banking on Ape's pink, fresh lungs, my own occasional Central Park jogging, to see me through.

Made 3rd-fastest time with milliseconds to spare. Duck, overawed, said he'd never seen me run like that before. He'd never seen me try before, I told him. (True, obviously—jogging or no jogging, I was still in Ape's body.)

At Morning Swim, my buddy Roland de Berganza, heir apparent to megabucks zinc fortune, was so condescendingly convinced waterskiing behind his family power launch on glassy Gulf of Mexico had to be superior to waterskiing behind rented speedboat (driven by Ellen) in choppy Long Island Sound, I felt obliged to challenge him that afternoon.

Chalk another one up for our team. In spite of wind and whitecaps on Soona Lake, passed Advanced status with swift shallow-water start and stunning standing stool-on-disc 360° turn; then topped off run by performing two requirements for Expert—sideslides and 180° back and fronts, vaulting me into top ten on ski ladder.

De Berganza, thanks to glassy Gulf of Mexico, nearly drowned.

Returned to Mount Olympus to peel off wet suit, blow nose (was this a cold coming on?), and accept congrats from all bunkmates except Duck, whose only comment was "You told me you hated waterskiing." (Is that so—how come he never told his father?)

"This is the new me," I said.

"Mmn," was the noncommittal response.

"What's eating you?" I asked.

"Oh, stuff," he said despondently.

"Like what?"

"Like this, for one." He handed me a padded manila envelope addressed to him from Galaxy.

I tipped it; out fell six transistor batteries.

"No accompanying letter or anything?" I asked, reaching around inside.

"I don't need a letter; I know it's from your Dad."

"Well, I need a letter and I was supposed to get one, too,"

I complained. "The Mailgram said 'detailed letter follows.' Follows what, I'd like to know—Christmas? Easter? It's Wednesday already."

"Not only do I not need a letter, I don't even need the batteries," said Duck morosely. "What good are batteries without the Sony?"

"Jeeze, I want to know what's going on out there, Duck!"

"It's just like *The Gift of the Magi,* remember *The Gift of the Magi?*"

It was conversational gridlock.

"You're not listening to a word I say," I said.

"Ditto to you," he answered. "And if you really want to know what's eating me—"

"Not especially. I'm much more interested in what we're eating for dinner," I said, and took off for the dining hall with de Menocal and Swensen.

In game room after dinner, was beaten by Duck, 21–15 in Ping-Pong, marking first defeat for our team. Luckily, no one of importance was around to see.

Later, signed up for Soonawissaclimbers' 2-day Katahdin trip. (Not willingly. Was egged on by Wilking's scathing recollection of my old man "bein' too yellow-bellied to set one foot front a the other less'n it was on flat ground"—no fool he!)

Thurs., July 7th, Fri., July 8th
Katahdin is highest mountain in Maine. If afraid of heights, don't look behind you. Forget about lost canteen—death by

127

dehydration is preferable to death by free fall. Besides, dehydration is impossible in Maine, it's The Land of the Summer Monsoon—a feature rarely disclosed in camp catalogues.

At 3 A.M., all eighteen of us abandoned floating pup tents, took refuge in hermetically sealed Reluctant Dragon, which normally seats twelve. No room, no air, no sleep.

Chalked up several more popularity points by regaling group with dirty jokes until dawn, when Wilking decided to cancel rest of trip and drove us back to camp. No fool he, either.

Spent rest of Fri. in infirmary with cold and low-grade fever, coughing up a storm, chalking up zilch. Still no mail. Day was total loss.

Sat., July 9th
Day was total triumph! Earned grudging respect from Wilking, gratitude from track team by demanding early release from infirmary in order to "win for Soonawissakit in the Intercamp Meet or die of pneumonia in the attempt."

Mission accomplished—a first in two out of three events, a tie for second in another!

Cough miraculously vanished—due, no doubt, to combination of youthful constitution and psychosomatic reaction to increasing popularity.

From here on in, could do no wrong, as evidenced by performance in late afternoon baseball game. I was 0 for 3 in the 7th (never was any good at that game), finally managed to connect with the ball—a rolling grounder straight to pitcher that should have made me 0 for 4 but pitcher made wild throw to first. Believe it or not, this was tactfully recorded as a base hit for me rather than an error for him!

After game, Swensen, #1 tennis player at camp, invited me to be his doubles partner in tourney semifinals the next day, substituting for #2 player, Gorsuch, who'd torn a ligament. Said he'd been impressed with how I'd pulled Levine's chestnuts out of the fire for him in the quarterfinals last Sunday and figured he and I would make a "ruhlly powerhouse combo."

I told him I'd like to, but was pretty much committed to Levine.

Swensen said he wouldn't want me to do anything scuzzy, conscience-wise, but since I'd never win with Levine anyway, if I could find some way to dump him, it would be ruhlly great.

Playing it ruhlly cool, I said I needed time to think about it and would let him know later. Actually, I'd made my decision the moment he asked me—it was only a question of implementing some ruhlly crafty strategy already forming in my ruhlly crafty mind.

After Dinner
"Hey, there, you two," I said to Annabel and Mallison at the track-meet victory bonfire. "Making out okay?"

Annabel hastily disengaged Mallison's arm from around her waist. "Is that your idea of sophisticated humor?" she said disparagingly.

"Oh, no—" I began.

"Then wipe the leer off your face," she warned.

"—I just wondered how you were making out," I said, continuing to leer.

"Not too bad, considering the lack of privacy around here," said Mallison with a salacious twinkle at Annabel.

She gave him an affectionate dig in the ribs. My fatherly blood began to boil. Clearly, they were making out just fine.

Stifling an impractical urge to tear Mallison apart with my bare hands, I stifled an ostentatious yawn instead. "Golly, between the track meet and the ballgame, I'm gonna hit the sack ruhlly early tonight. I bet our whole cabin will—except poor Duck, of course. He has one heckuva time falling asleep without that Sony. . . ."

Later That Night

Mallison, making his escape from the conked-out cabin, stopped by Duck's bed for a second.

"Enjoy," he whispered. Then he left.

"Enjoy what?" said Duck. "Another sleepless night?"

"This," I said, handing him the Sony. "And the batteries still work, Mallison said so."

"Ape, oh, Ape," he crooned ecstatically. "How did you get him to do it?"

"It was kind of a trade-off. My sister for your transistor, as it were." I sighed.

"Knowing how you feel about your sister, that was an incredible sacrifice."

"Knowing how you feel about your music, it was worth it." The moment was ripe. "Duck, I'm dumping you for Swensen in the semis tomorrow. I hope you don't mind."

No answer from Duck. So much for the ruhlly crafty strategy. I wasn't about to sacrifice my daughter for nothing, however.

"The thing is, with Swensen, I think I have a crack at winning the whole thing. I hope you don't mind," I said again.

"Under the circumstances, what can I say," said Duck in such a neutral tone I couldn't get an accurate reading on it.

"You could say I was a rat-fink deserter," I suggested humbly.

"No, I couldn't. I could never say that about you, Ape," said Duck loyally. "Go ahead, play with Swensen. It doesn't make that much difference to me. If it does to you . . . well . . ." He clapped his beloved headphones on and rolled over. "Just make sure you win."

Sun., July 10th
We won all right. Wiped the court with them, in fact (6–2, 6–0), and since one of them was Roland de Berganza, born with a silver sneaker in his mouth, the victory was sweet indeed.

Sweeter still was the weekly awards ceremony after dinner, when I was presented with a plaque proclaiming me Soonawissacamper of the Week.

To the Greater Glory of Ape Face! I thought to myself as I raised the plaque high above my head. I did it for our team, rah-rah-rah!

But then, as I was being carried out of the dining room on the shoulders of my newfound friends and admirers amidst cheers and huzzahs from the exultant throng, a startling thought occurred to me:

I hadn't done it for our team and the Greater Glory of Ape Face. There *was* no our team; there was only my team and the Greater Glory of Me. Because Ape Face and I were probably never going to change back.

Or had I subconsciously suspected that all along? I wonder. . . .

Fifteen

(continued from July 5th)

Today, Sun., July 10th, it's 96° and so smoggy at the pool I can hardly see to write. I bet the air in Maine is much better—this stuff really burns your eyes.

Anyway, sorry for the delay, but the whole week has been a madhouse.

Wed. and Thurs. were full of meetings, screenings, and the usual dailies in the afternoon. Having to watch the same scene over and over again got pretty

interesting on Thursday when we had to watch a man and a woman take off all their clothes and make love in a wheat field over and over again.

boring after a while, but don't worry, I didn't ho-hum any more than anyone else.

Quite a lot less, in fact. In fact, being someone who usually has to get a grown-up to walk me into an R-rated flick, it was all I could do not to oh-wow! through the whole thing.

> Wed. night was the weekly dinner meeting (catered at the studio) when all the top brass sit around discussing their projects. I handled it very well considering

considering what?. . . Considering I didn't know what any of my projects were and your friend Tony "The Shunner" Crane kept pressing me on production details in order to show me up? I can't put that in, Duck might read it. But I sure would like to know what Dad ever did to him, the guy's a real snake. . . .

> I'm new at the job.
> Of course, it helps having Stephanie (Marshak—we're on a first-name basis, isn't everybody?) in my corner.
> Speaking of Stephanie, guess what?! Remember that Miss Moon who taught you 2nd and 3rd grade, the one you pretended not to like because I didn't approve of her too much? Well, that's *Stephanie!*—what a coincidence! I cer-

tainly approve of her now, and not just
because she's my boss, either.

So there, Daddio!

Then, beginning on Thurs., late aft

Boy, was that only last Thursday? So much has happened since then; there's been a kind of real change in
me since then—no, no, it's not what you think, I'm still
6'1" with a beard* and everything, it's nothing anyone
looking at me could put a finger on, nothing physical,
I mean, but since last Thursday . . .

I began looking at houses for us to
live in.

I guess it was the houses that did it, the houses
and the schools. Between Thursday and Saturday, I
saw twenty-three rich houses†, eight schools, and every

---

* I noticed this morning it's getting scraggly again but it's Sunday
  and the barber is closed. Maybe I'll shave the whole thing
  off—messing around with it's a royal pain.
† Harvey Godchaux told me on Wednesday the details of my
  deal were all worked out, and I should be thinking in the
  seven-fifty or slightly higher range.
    "Dollars a month?" I asked.
    "What are you, crazy? That'd get you a kennel for your
  keeshond!" (Everybody out here has dogs you never heard of.)
  "I'm talking about purchase price. In thou's." Gulp!

street, drive, boulevard, canyon, and hairpin curve in the greater Los Angeles area.

By Saturday night at Peggotty Horn's party—which was a combination Sweet Sixteen Come As Your Favorite Horror Film Hero/Heroine party for her daughter Melanie Sue and a Come As You Are party for everyone else in Hollywood—I was so confused and worried, all I could do was sit on a satin couch in front of the fireplace and stare into the fake flames (fueled by a gas jet underneath an asbestos log).

"Hey, chum, mind if I join you?"

I looked up. It was Ty Donovan.

"Heck, no, why should I mind? Sit down," I said, glad to see him. "How's it going?" Duck usually levels with me the second time around.

"Like I said, great," said Ty, still on automatic pilot.

I guess it was dumb of me to ask. What did I expect him to say? "Lousy? Everything's going lousy! Nothing good is ever going to happen to me ever again, I just know it!"—which is the way he looked. The big guys don't talk to each other like that.

"Well, if there's anything I can do . . ." I said vaguely, which was as personal as I thought I could get.

"Nothing. Unless you run across a hot property you want to shoot my way," he said.

"Sure thing," I said.

"How's by you?" he asked. "Feeling a little more on top of it than the last time I saw you?"

"Absolutely." I can play this stupid game, too, Ty baby. You're the one who taught me how. "Things absolutely couldn't be better."

". . . Because if you ever need a sympathetic ear . . ." He paused, studied the ice in his drink, jiggled it around, then looked up and straight at me. "Listen, Bill, about what I said the other day, forget it. I was just—you know, bruised-feelings department. I mean you really can trust me, I really am your friend."

"And I'm yours, Ty."

We both sounded so sincere, you'd certainly think we were friends.

Well maybe we are . . .

"Bill," said Ty, lowering his voice, "a word of warning, look out for Tony Crane."

. . . but maybe we aren't. For all I know, he's Tony *Crane's* friend.

"No kidding," I said cautiously. "I've only had a couple of meetings with him, but so far so good. He seems like a nifty guy."

All the warmth went out of Ty's face. "Okay, chum, I tried," he said, rising, "but if that's the way you want to play it, to each his own." He looked away from me.

But it isn't! I don't want to play anything. I feel like a rat chasing my own tail! "Wait a minute, Ty!"

"Ty who?" said a voice behind me.

I turned. It was Ray Ewald. "Ty Donovan," I said quickly, and turned back again but it was too late, he'd been swallowed up by the crowd.

"Is he a friend of yours?" asked Ray.

The moment of truth.

"He used to be," I said, "but I don't know if he still is."

"Just as well," said Ray. "He's a loser anyway."

"But I *hope* he still is," I said fiercely.

"Hanging out with losers isn't too swift an idea, Willy," said good old Ray.

"To each his own," I said. "What's your idea of a winner—him, I suppose?" I jerked a thumb at Tony Crane making points with Peggotty Horn at the bar.

"Now you're talking," said Ray. "Or her," he said, waving at Miss Moon across the room.

I made a beeline for her. She seemed as pleased to see me as I was to see her.

"Bill! I didn't even know you were here!" She clutched my arm impulsively. "What a zoo!"

"You should see the children's zoo downstairs," I told her. "There was a girl standing around in a long white dress completely covered with blood all over her face and everything—very yuck—having a friendly conversation with a boy with an axe—presumably the one who did it to her.

"'Boy,' I thought, 'if someone hacked me up like that, I sure wouldn't be standing around having a friendly chat, I'd be dead on the floor, and why wasn't she?'

"Then I found out she was Carrie from *Carrie,* which I never saw, and he was Jason from *Friday the 13th* Parts One and Two, which I also never saw because my mom wouldn't let me—" WATCH IT! "—take her (I have this nice old mom I take to the movies but she doesn't like the scary ones), and the two of them went together in real life."

"Real life," said Miss Moon as she surveyed the scene, "is pretty unreal sometimes."

Oh, Miss Moon, you don't know the half of it!

"Say, do you want to sit down somewhere with me?" I asked eagerly. "I need your advice on a few things."

She was willing, so we sat on the satin couch in front of the fake fire and I told her about all the houses and how I couldn't decide among them.

Hadn't I been able to eliminate any of them? she asked. Weren't there one or two that shrieked, "Buy me! Buy me!" as soon as I walked through the door?

"That's the trouble, there are three like that," I told her. "There's the one in Pacific Palisades—top of San Remo Drive. A little expensive but a terrific view, huge swimming pool, *two* Jacuzzis, *and* a paddle-tennis court which Dad would love—"

The look on her face stopped me.

"—to play on when he comes to visit with my old mom."

"Remarkably spry, that old man of yours," said Miss Moon.

"Oh, yes, fit as anything," I agreed. What's the matter with me tonight!—I keep forgetting who I am! "Then there's a house on Mulholland. The price is right, and it has a great kitchen—built-in convertible microwave oven, compacter, white glass chopping-block counter, center island with top burners, charcoal grill—"

"Do you cook a lot?" she asked.

"No, but—"

"Your old mom does?" she suggested, grinning.

I nodded. "Yes, and so does my wife. My wife would like that Mulholland house very much. It even has an earthquake room."

"Ah, but how does your wife feel about earthquakes? Because Mulholland Drive . . ." she trailed off dubiously.

That was part of my problem, I explained. On account of my wife was still away and I couldn't check it out with her.

"But then there's the house in Westwood. I *love* Westwood. It's only twenty minutes from the beach, but it's like, I dunno, it's like . . ."

"New York," offered Miss Moon.

"Right! Record shops, pizza, movies, arcades, Adidas, ice-cream parlors—"

"I know, I know," laughed Miss Moon. "That's why I live there."

"No! Do you?"

"For now," she said. "But I'll have to move soon, I'm afraid. It's not"—she made a mocking face—"a suitable area for the president of Galaxy."

"According to the real-estate agent, it's not even a suitable area for a vice-president of Galaxy," I said.

"Supposedly not," said Miss Moon. "But if the house is nice, what do you care? How's the house?"

"Great! Great, *great* house. Not so jazzy kitchen-wise or poolwise—postage-stamp pool, and no tennis court or paddle tennis, but a game room that won't quit. Giant wall TV, billiard table, pinball, jukebox, Space Invaders all included in the purchase price." CAREFUL! "My son would *love* that house."

There was never any point in trying to fool Miss Moon. "Your son, Bill, or you?" she said skeptically. "Come on, now, the truth."

So I gave it to her. "Me, I guess. Sounds silly, but I love those kid games."

"Then that's the house for you."

". . . But now that I think about it, my son might want something more status-y, Bev Hills maybe, or that Pacific Palisades house—"

"Oh, Bill, you make me impatient, honestly you do! You're so worried about what everybody else wants—what do *you* want?"

"What do *I* want?"

That all depends on who "I" is. If I'm Ape Face only temporarily in possession of Dad's body, then I

141

have to make decisions he can live with when he repossesses himself—which isn't so easy because I don't know who he is either. (A first banana would go for status; a second banana posing as a first banana probably would, too. A regular, nonpretending second banana might care as much about pleasing his family as himself, but Mom likes kitchens and I like game rooms. . . . Knowing Dad, we'd end up on Mulholland with the microwave, and I really *love* that game room. . . .)

On the other hand, if "I" is Ape Face in permanent possession of Dad's body—

"Hello?" Miss Moon waved her hand in front of my face.

I came to.

"Good, you're still alive," she said, amused.

"Sorry. What do *I* want?"

"Yes, Bill." She smiled into my eyes. "What do you want?"

"I want . . ." My stomach turned over, I could hear my heart beating. "I want . . ." to kiss Miss Moon. I want Miss Moon to kiss me. I want, oh I want—

"Are we interrupting something?"

It was Millicent Ewald on the arm of Ray.

Without taking her eyes from mine, Miss Moon said gently, firmly, with a tiny shake of her head, "No."

Then she directed her attention to the Ewalds and talked about my housing dilemma. Or I guess that's what it was. You can hear words but it's hard to grasp their meaning when everything inside you has gone so suddenly still as death. There was talk about Ellen . . .? Okay, I think I said. Talk about thought maybe we were separated? What? I said. . . . Separated? . . . Yes. No! She's in Window Rock, Arizona . . . for long? . . . I don't know, maybe. . . .

After a while I gave up. Said good night. Found Barkham. Went home to the hotel. Looked at myself in the mirror for a long, long time. Then reached out and touched the image of my face. Don't be sad, I told myself. At least now you know what it feels like—loving. That's something, anyway. And tomorrow, I lifted my chin, tomorrow . . .

I'm about to close a deal on a super house in Westwood because after looking at a bunch of them, I've decided it's definitely the one I want.

As for schools, I plan to sign you up for Wormley—it's very achievement oriented, you'll like it a lot, I'm sure, and you can be dropped off there on my way to the studio.

Gee whiz, Soonawissavisitors' Day is less than a week away. I haven't talked to Mom, but she can't be any more anxious to see you than I am.

"Mr. Andrews? They just announced a telephone call for you, Mr. Andrews. Didn't you hear?"

"No, but thanks," I said, looking up. It was the same middle-aged bellboy with the paunch who'd delivered my bags that first day.

"Hey, I've been looking for you ever since I arrived!" I said, digging out a fiver from the toe of my Gucci. "Here you go, and if you'll just wait a sec . . ."

I hastily scribbled Love, Dad, jammed the letter into an already-addressed envelope, and handed it to him with instructions to have it go out immediately.

Then I hippety-hopped my way over all the glistening bodies to the poolside phone.

"Hello?" I said.

"Hi, darling," said a very-long-distance voice.

"Mom!" I exclaimed happily. "Where are you?!"

Nowhere, apparently.

"Are you still there?" I asked.

I heard her clear her throat. Good. She was still there.

"This must be a horrible connection," she said. "I thought you said, 'Hi, Mom.'"

"Oh-ho-ha-ha-ho-ho-ho-ho-ho-ho!" I laughed— probably the longest laugh in history, also the phoniest, but it gave me time to think. "Not Mom, *Tom* is what I said. Tom is a cute little kid I play with out here at the pool.

"Not now, Tom," I said, off phone, shooing him

away. "I'm talking long distance to my wife. Go play by yourself, g'wan, git!"

Two glistening bikini bods raised themselves up on oily elbows to look for Phantom Tom. Not finding him, they whispered to each other about me (not very subtly, either), then slid back down their elbows to broil themselves some more.

"Sorry about that, Ellen," I said. "Now tell me everything. How goes it in Window Rock, *are* you in Window Rock? I thought they didn't have phones on your reservation."

They didn't, said Mom. She wasn't there anymore, she was in Tucson because she was through, through, *through*—wasn't that exciting!—earlier than she'd expected. And how was I, darling?

Darling told her all about the promotion, and about the funny coincidence of *Ben's* teacher (this time I got it right) being my boss, and then, because I knew I couldn't put it off much longer, I tackled Topic A.

"I have great news for you," I said. "A wonderful house in Westwood."

"What wonderful house in Westwood?"

"A wonderful house for us. Or will be. The kitchen needs a small amount of fixing but there's a great ga—"

"Bill"—her voice had a sharp edge to it—"if you're saying what I think you're saying, you'd better not be."

"I was afraid of that," I groaned. "Well, there's another house on Mulholland that does have a great kitchen but I thought you weren't so interested in cooking now that you're working—"

"In New York!" she shouted. "I am working in New York, not in California. Are you out of your mind?!"

"But *Mom*," Jeeze! "*Tom,* will you cut that out, get away from me now, no more tickling!"

The bikini bods oozed upright, and watched me closely from under their pitch-black shades.

I covered the phone and explained myself. "It's dotty old Mom, she thinks my older brother's still alive—died years ago of—" what did people die of years ago? "diphtheria, poor Tom—but we have to keep pretending—"

Do I care what they think? Phooey on them. "Ellen," I said into the phone, "Ellen, listen to me—"

"Now he's calling her Ellen," observed Bikini Bod #1.

"Mad as a March hare," said B.B. #2.

Double phooey on them!

"No, you listen to me," she said, and for several fun-filled minutes, she let me have it right between the eyes about the scarcity of museum jobs and how hard she'd worked to get this one, and what did I think she was anyway that I could unplug her in one place and plug her in someplace else without even asking— a portable TV? I hadn't heard her that mad since the day I wouldn't eat Annabel's Sugar Coated Snappy Crackles because I didn't want to make *her* mad (you know how I am), and that was years ago. (Also a whole other story, which I won't tell now.)

But after I said I was sorry about twelve times, she finally calmed down. And then it got worse.

"Not as sorry as I am," she said in this lethally quiet voice. "You see, I thought we had a partnership going for us, but nowadays, I'm the kid in the mailroom and you're the chairman of the board—pardon me, Executive Vice President in Charge of Worldwide Production, *bucking* for chairman of the board—"

"Don't be mean!"

"Don't interrupt—and at the rate you're going, you'll probably make it, too, although I'm not sure I want to be around when it happens."

I let out a squawk of protest which she rode roughshod right over.

"—Because frankly, Bill, you're just not the same man I married."

I'm not? "What do you mean?"

"Aw, come on, Willy," she said angrily, "who needs a movie mogul? I want my nice, vulnerable," what's so great about vulnerable that everybody loves it so much? "struggling young writer back!"

Dad started as a writer? How about that!

"But aside from the writer part, you're describing me exactly," I said. Me and Dad both, I suddenly realized. Alike! The same! How about THAT! "That's exactly who I am. Exactly!"

"I don't think you know who you are," she said, sounding serious and sad and determined. "When you find out, I hope you'll let me know."

Was that a click?

"Mom . . . Tom? . . . Ellen?"

Definitely a click.

Oh Lord, now what?!

Behind my back, I heard the bikini bods discussing me.

"I think his girl friend just hung up on him"—B.B. #1.

"Why couldn't it be his wife just hung up on him?"—B.B. #2.

"If it was his wife, he wouldn't have tried to fool us in the beginning by calling her Mom"—B.B. #1.

"He didn't call her Mom, he called her Tom. Maybe it was a boyfriend just hung up on him"—B.B. #2.

"He also called her Ellen"—B.B. #1.

"If he called her Ellen, it was his wife—but not for long, honey, not for long. Splitsville, I hear"—B.B. #3(!!).

"Bull!" I said, facing them. "We're just having a few problems, that's all."

"I know," said B.B. #3, a.k.a. Millicent Ewald.

Just my luck!

Sixteen

". . . Sperling, de Menocal, Belknap, Loring . . ." Letty "Ma Barker" Newsome was handing out mail, "Von Volkening, Hitzigger . . ." to everyone but me, naturally—why should this day (Wednesday) be different from any other? ". . . Beaty, Levine . . ."

Duck's parents wrote constantly. If a neurosurgeon can find time, what's the matter with a film executive, he's got a secretary, hasn't he? What's the matter with "Hello, how are you?" dictated to a secretary? Fine father he's going to make!

". . . Swensen, Gorsuch, Andrews—"

Well, whaddya know! Finally! I leaped forward.

"*Annabel* Andrews," clarified Ma Barker.

I fell back—into Annabel, who elbowed me aside, quipping, "Is your name Annabel?" (Ever since the day I made Soonawissacamper of the Week, or around about then, she'd begun being quite uncordial, I don't know why. Maybe she's the kind of foul-weather friend who only loves a loser.)

"A postcard from Mom," she announced smugly, whipping it under my nose too fast to read.

"O'Neal, e-a, O'Neill, e-i, Andrews, Ben . . ."

The A Group (Hitzigger, Swensen, Biddle, etc. plus Duck—a probationary member in on my coattails, so to speak), burst into happy applause for me.

"I suppose you got one, too," said Annabel, worried I was going to do her one better.

"A postcard from Mom *and* a fat letter from Dad!" I said, doing her one better.

"Bully for you," she said. (Annabel as a daughter is merely a continuing responsibility. Annabel as a sister stinks!)

I sat down on a stump and opened Dad's—my *son's* letter.

"What does he say?" asked Annabel, eagerly leaning over me.

I shifted positions so she couldn't see. "Is your name Ape Face?" Sibling rivalry is a two-way street, kiddo!

> Dear Ape Face,
>   How's camp? Fine, I'll bet. That's good. I'm

"Boy, is he boring!" said Duck over my left shoulder.

I whipped around and glared at him. "Are you usually in the habit of reading other people's mail?"

"Yours, I am," he said, injured. "You always let me."

"Oh." In that case, there wouldn't be anything in this about Us, nothing that wasn't safe for Duck to read.

"Well, okay then," I told him. "But not you," I told Annabel.

While she stood by, seething with impatience, Duck and

I skimmed the next few sentences about having fun at camp and California weather, blah, blah, blah.

"Boring isn't the word for it, it's the terminal big Z's," I complained to Duck.

"I guess he just writes the way he talks," said Duck.

"How do you know how he talks?" I said, highly offended. "You only met him once."

"Yes, but you told me a million times—"

"Told you what? What did I tell you?"

"Oh, you know," said Duck. "About how every day he asks you how was school? and you say fine, and he says that's good—don't you remember telling me that? And then one day you got so sick of the same dumb conversation, when he said how was school, you said fine except the tip of your finger got cut off in the jigsaw and you fed it to the guinea pig—"

Annabel let out a whoop of laughter. "Ape, you didn't! That's hysterical!"

"—and your father said that's good, because he wasn't even listening?" finished Duck.

Annabel's face fell. "Oh," she gasped. "Oh, no, that's awful!"

"Yes," I said, embarrassed. "It really is."

The realization that Ape's boring letter was actually a skillful parody of my own boringness made me blush all over.

Annabel put her arm around me. "Don't worry, Ape, he does things like that to me, too, sometimes. He means well, he just gets sort of—"

"Preoccupied," I suggested. "Very preoccupied with very demanding work."

"Yeah, right," she said loyally. Atta girl, Annabel! not such a bad sister/daughter/whichever, after all.

As a peace offering, I allowed her to read over my right shoulder while Duck continued reading over my left.

"Hey, listen to this!" Annabel snatched the letter away from me and read aloud the section on the Moon/Marshak revelation.

Learning that Moon was Marshak held no particular significance for me since I couldn't remember having met her in the first place. (School is Ellen's department—or was in those early days before she got involved in anthropology and I took over some of her responsibilities—well, I suppose they're partially my responsibilities, too. . . .)

"But I can't believe I'd pretend not to like someone just because Dad didn't approve of her," I said.

"*I* can!" said Annabel and Duck together.

"You're scared to death of Dad and you know it," said Annabel, adding complacently, "I don't know why."

"Neither do I." If true, though, it was a rather unsettling notion. As for the bit about "I certainly approve of her now, and not just because she's my boss, either"—was I being hypersensitive or was Ape Face, having already implied that I was a remote, uninterested and intimidating father, now zinging it to me for being an opportunistic *hypocrite?* If so, that was even more unsettling.

And you ain't heard nothing yet, folks!

"What's this about houses?" mumbled Annabel, reading on. "Whoop-de-doo-de-doo!" she hooted. "We're moving to California!"

I snatched the letter back, scanned it frantically. "Where does it say that? Where, where, where?! I don't see anything about California."

Duck pointed to the sentence about Westwood. I read it once, then I read it again, and then I was outraged!

"How *dare* he! How does he know I want to move to California, maybe I do and maybe I don't! And what makes him think I want to live in Westwood, that's a ridiculous place for a vice-president to live, I'd rather live in Brentwood—"

"You're not vice-president, Dad is," said Annabel.

"Button up, missy, that's enough out of you!" I shouted.

"*Now* listen to him," she said to Duck scornfully. "He's even talking like Dad."

"That's right, that's right, I am! And I'm thinking like him, too, since he's too stupid and incompetent to think for himself—"

"Lawsy, *lawsy* me!" said Annabel. I wanted to wring her neck.

"—but if he could, let me tell you something, young lady, he wouldn't think much of your behavior this summer, you're an absolute disgrace, you and that goat Mallison sneaking around in the middle of the night doing heaven knows what—"

"It's none of your ever-loving business what we do, you little creep, but for your information, we don't do anything."

"Aw, gee," said Duck, "why not?"

"Another county heard from." Annabel rolled her eyes. "Because I've decided he's not my type, we're just friends."

"I don't believe a word of it," I declared. I didn't!

"I don't give a rat's ear *what* you believe, it's true!"

"And even if it *is* true," I went on, "between sneaking around in private and necking in public, you two are abrogating your responsibility to provide decent role models for impressionable youngsters, which is something I certainly don't approve of, as you well know—so why are you looking at me like that Annabel"—she had a very peculiar expression on her face—"I've made myself clear on this issue many times before, have I not?"

"No, you have not," she said, narrowing her eyes in thought, "but Dad has."

"Annabel," said Duck, out of the side of his mouth, "I think he thinks he's your father."

This was getting a little too close for comfort.

"Don't be dumb. I know perfectly well who I am," I said, storking to prove it.

"You're sure?" Annabel was suspicious, I could tell.

"Sure, I'm sure," I said, losing my balance and crashing to the ground.

"Ape Face," she said tactfully as she helped me up again, "how would you like to go to the nice infirmary?"

"I wouldn't," I said. "I'm fine."

"Well," she said, linking her arm firmly through mine, "you seem a bit upset."

"Of *course* I'm upset," I said, shaking her arm loose. "Why

154

wouldn't I be upset! Not one word out of that jerk for ten lousy days while I molder away in this crummy hole wondering what's going on, and suddenly it's Dear Ape Face, how are you, I'm fine, bingo, bango, guess what, we're moving to California, I bought a house in Westwood. *WESTWO-O-OD!*" I howled like a wolf. "He's got some bloody nerve. He can't make decisions like that without consulting me!"

After a second of strained silence, Duck ventured a timid question. "Why not?"

"Yes, why not?" Annabel chimed in. "Who *do* you think you are, might I ask?"

"That's beside the point!"

"No, it isn't, Ape. It's exactly the point," said Duck, hoping to get through to me with reason and logic. "After all, you're only a kid."

He couldn't possibly have said anything worse.

"Now *there's* a clever observation!" I smirked.

"Cool it, Ape," said Annabel, protecting Duck.

She needn't have bothered. His response was to stare at me for so long and with such open hostility, I was forced to look away. Back I went to the letter, to another charming surprise.

"Now hear this," I said, attempting a reconciliation. "If you're interested, that is."

Annabel shrugged.

"Suit yourself," said Duck.

"'As for schools, I plan to sign you up for Wormley—it's very achievement oriented, you'll like it a lot, I'm sure.' What makes him so sure?"

"Maybe he's heard about the New You," said Duck acidly, and walked away.

"Another foul-weather friend," I remarked, watching him go.

"Meaning?" asked Annabel.

"Meaning he liked me better when I was an oddball like him. And I suppose you did, too," I said accusingly.

"Ape," she said, evading the issue, "you haven't read your postcard from Mom. Here." She patted the stump, we both sat down, "give it over, I'll read it to you.

" 'Darling Ben, Work at Window Rock went wonderfully, completed research ahead of schedule and decided to stop off in L.A. to visit Dad for a few days—' "

I slapped the postcard out of her hand. "She can't!" I brayed. "She was going to fly straight here, that was always the plan!"

"Well, now it isn't," said Annabel unflappably. "Now she's going to have an impromptu two-day honeymoon with Dad first."

"No honeymoon! That's out of the question!" I screamed. And I mean screamed. Alarmed birds flew out of the bushes, Ma Barker stuck her head out of the infirmary window to see what was going on. Annabel gave her a signal indicating 'scram, everything was under control, which it most decidedly was not.

"Brother mine," soothed Annabel, "you are a classic little-boy basket case in love with his mother—"

"I am *not* in love with my mother!"

"—which is a stage all little boys go through, just the way all little girls are in love with their fathers and I used to be in love with Dad—"

"—And now you're in love with Terry Mallison." I scowled at her.

"God almighty, Ape Face, you've got to be the only kid in the world in love with his mother *and* his sister! Sick, sick, sick!"

"Finish the postcard, will you please, doctor."

"Finish it yourself," she said, picking it up off the ground and tossing it in my lap. "I'm going for a walk."

    . . . but the museum director wants me back
    in New York, so there goes that!
Good!
      Cannot *wait* for Saturday. I've missed
    you, love you, Mom

Mom . . . Good-bye, Ellen, hello *Mom*?! *Forever*?! It was unthinkable. So unthinkable, I'd avoided thinking about it altogether.

But you really must, I told myself. You've got to begin at the beginning and think it through, *all* through. From the beginning . . .

Well then: I have been given (by whom and for whatever reasons I suppose I'll never know) a new lease on life, which in my case means the chance to become what everybody, even Ellen, already believes me to be: Willy Winner. Let's hear it for Willy Winner!

"If I'd only known then what I know now," people are

always saying. Okay. For me, Then has become Now, and Now will become thirty brand-new, born-again years to whip the world into shape (funny word, whip—is that what I mean?)—how bad can that be? I'm already number-one jock in the camp and I betrayed my best friend in the bargain—congratulations, Willy, you're on your way.

Another crack at Varsity track, another crack at college boards, college interviews—Yale this time around. Do they still have Freshman mixers?—poised, this time around. Do they still have senior dances?—who this time around? Who do I take? Anybody I want, they all want me. I want Ellen. Not this time around.

But I want Ellen. To sit across the dinner table, to share the little triumphs and sometimes little losses. To love me and to love. *Not this time around.*

I want to walk my daughter down the aisle. But I'm not going to be the father of the bride. I'm going to be the brother of the bride, this time around.

I want to be a wiser, kinder father to my son. Too late, Willy Winner, too late . . .

I cried, then. Alone on a stump (in full view of nobody, thank God), the Soonawissacamper of the Week cried—isn't that something? Cried buckets for the thirty misbegotten years that lay ahead and the thirty irretrievably behind.

Seventeen

Every once in a while there's a day that starts off so badly, things can only get worse because one bad thing leads to another. I'm talking about Thursday, July 14th.

It started off with the *Today* show on in the bedroom and me in the bathroom, an English muffin on one side of the sink, o-juice on the other, trying to decide whether or not to shave off my beard.

On the basis of having nothing better to do at that moment, plus it was costing me a fortune at the barber, and I was bored with being told by everybody I met about the bit of this or that nesting in it (Frosted Flakes being the worst offender, bacon-cheddar cheeseburger remnants runner-up), I decided to go ahead.

I should have decided not to. Getting rid of a big tough beard with a puny electric razor is almost impossible. What you need is a machete, which I didn't happen to have. There was hair all over the bathroom, floating in the o-juice, sprinkled on the muffin—a surprising amount, really, when you consider how much

159

of it was still on my face, looking as though rodents had nibbled at it during the night.

This is a gosh-darn mess, I said to myself. (Well, that's approximately it—what I actually said was a good deal shorter. One word, actually.)

From the bathroom phone, I rang the barber downstairs and humbly asked his advice. To go snip-snip with a nice sharp scissors first and *then* zippety-zap with the razor was his advice—why didn't I come in and let him do the job properly?

Because that would make me late for my 9:15 meeting at the studio with my boss, but thank you any-way, I told him—and tackled the job myself.

Bulletin: Scissors—the kind that come in the handy travel sewing kit your wife packs for you—are not nice and sharp; they are nice and blunt. Toenail clippers are nice and sharp, but short—only a half inch of cutting edge, and ever so slightly rounded down-ward at either end (so you won't get an ingrown toe-nail). This makes them perfect for toes but slow going for beards because after every half-inch snip, you then have to snip off the tufts the clippers missed at either end (but you won't get an ingrown beard).

By 8:40 (twenty-five infuriating minutes later), I was finally finished snipping and about to start zippety-zapping when Peggotty Horn began her daily hatchet job on—who would it be this morning? I wondered, razor poised in midair.

You'll never guess.

"A sorrowful little bird tells me that Galaxy's vice-prexy Bill Andrews and his lovely wife, Ellen, designer of Navajo jewelry," Mom'll love that! "are definitely splitsville."

"No, no, no!" I yelled and slammed the bathroom door.

In a rage, I picked up the electric razor, and imagining I was dismembering Piggotty Peggotty and her sorrowful little bird, a.k.a. Millicent the Buzzard, into itty-bitty bite-sized pieces to feed to the polar pears, I viciously whacked, hacked, pulled, tugged, yanked, and gouged away at myself until I was completely clean-shaven—and looked as though I'd been run over by a threshing machine.

For the next part of the day, on top of everything else, I suffered from an acute identity crisis, beginning in the hotel lobby.

Nobody down there knew me. De Virgilio passed me by completely, so did Malcolm the maitre d', Miss Vondermuhl, and even the middle-aged bellboy, who after my five-dollar tip had every reason to not only know me but love me. And at the front door, when I asked Doorman Bob if I could have my car, please, his answer was what car, sir?

"That car," I said pointing to Barkham and the Mercedes parked a few yards away.

"That is Mr. Andrews' car, sir," he said.

I started to tell him I was Mr. Andrews, but Doorman Bob, having already dismissed me as a nobody, was deep in conversation with a somebody. To heck with this, I thought, if Muhammad won't come to the mountain, et cetera, and marched to the car alone.

Barkham was engrossed in the London *Times*. I rapped on the window to get his attention and started to open the door, but after one quick glimpse of me he pushed the automatic door-lock button.

"Let me in, will you? I'm late already," I told him.

"This car is reserved for Mr. Andrews," he said in his hoity-toitiest voice, deliberately omitting the sir. (A chauffeur is never unintentionally rude.)

"Barkham, it's *me*," I said. "Minus the beard, that's all."

Barkham leaped out of the car and solicitously guided me in.

"Well, sir, I must say, sir," he said with a hollow cackle, "you look as though you'd had a bit of a run-in with the Demon Barber of Fleet Street."

"Very funny," I said, slumping in my seat.

Barkham eyed me edgily in the rearview mirror. "There are tissues right behind you, sir." He swerved to avoid collision with a Porsche. "Mind the uphol-stery!" Mind the upholstery! I'll kill him! (Or he'll kill me.)

"Forget the upholstery, mind the road!" I yelped, trying to preserve what remained of my mutilated self in case Dad ever moved back in.

"As you wish, sir," replied Barkham stiffly—the last words he uttered until we reached the Galaxy gate, where he had to identify me to Miguel the guard, who also didn't recognize me, and neither did my very own secretary, Mavis Ohler. Honestly!

Frankly, the whole thing was getting to be incredibly ridiculous and humiliating; furthermore, my face hurt, and I was upset about Peggotty Horn and worried about my mother, and as for Betty Lou Bienenstock, she was the last straw.

"Excuse me, sir," she said as I headed for Miss Moon's office. "Sir! Where do you think you're going?"

"In," I said, my hand on the doorknob.

"Well, I'm very sorry," she said, not sounding sorry at all, "but Miss Marshak never sees anyone without a prior appointment—if you'd care to leave your name . . ."

"My name?! My name," I said, fighting for control, "is William," pause, "Waring," pause, "Andrews. And I *have* a prior appointment"—I tapped my watch impatiently—"which you are making me late for!"

Then, before there were any further protests, I barged right in and closed the door behind me.

"Sorry, I'm late," I said.

Miss Moon looked at me puzzled. "Don't I know you from somewhere?"

"Yes. I shaved off my beard."

"With a grapefruit spoon, evidently."

I forced a painful smile. "Might as well have been."

She was still looking at me puzzled, so I refreshed her memory. "Bill Andrews, V.P. in Charge of Worldwide Production, fellow New Yorker."

She laughed. "Bill, I know who you are. But why do you suddenly look so familiar?"

Because among your other virtues, you are someone who *really* never forgets a face and you saw mine, unbearded, once in the second grade—but I don't want to get into that now.

"Beats me," I told her. "Listen, I know we're supposed to talk about future projects, but I want to talk about something else."

"Such as," said Miss Moon warily.

"Such as did you hear what Peggotty Horn said this morning on the *Today* show?"

"Oh, that," she said, breathing a sigh of relief. "According to Peggotty Horn, half the couples in L.A. are splitsville—I wouldn't be upset about that, if I were you."

"No? Well, I am. Very. Extremely."

She took off her aviator glasses. "Mm," she said thoughtfully. "Bill, if it's not too personal, would you mind telling me, are you upset because you and your wife *are* splitsville, or because you aren't?"

"Yes. No! I don't know. Both, I think. I'm all confused."

"That makes two of us," said Miss Moon. "Enlighten me. Have a seat." She pointed to the desk chair. "Take it from the top."

"Okay," I said, sitting, "but it's kind of a long story, do you have time?"

"No, but I'll make time," she said. That's Miss Moon for you—she always makes time when it's important, and miraculously, she always seems to sense when it will be.

Gratefully, I began. "Remember that first day when you asked didn't I want to check it out with my wife before I said yes to a West Coast job, and I said no, we had an old-fashioned marriage, she went where I went? Well, I should have said yes—I mean yes to the check-out, no to the job, because you see my wife has her own job—at the Museum of Natural History—"

"Which she doesn't want to leave, naturally." Miss Moon was not a bit surprised.

"No. In fact, when I talked to her on the phone in Tucson last Sunday, she was so mad at me for not taking her job into consideration, I think right now she'd rather leave me than it. And I don't know what to do."

Tell me what to do, Miss Moon, come on, tell me! But she wouldn't.

"Bill," she said, shaking her head, "here we go again, it's just like the houses. Granted, choosing between career and marriage is a slightly stickier wicket . . ." She briefly contemplated the problem, then made a suggestion. "What about your plan to commute back and forth?"

"I didn't even get a chance to suggest it—she hung *up* on me! But she'd never go for that, I know she wouldn't. What am I going to do?"

Please, Miss Moon? Just one little hint.

"Friend," she said, folding her hands on the desk, "what do you *want* to do?"

Push, push, push! I can't take much more of this.

"It all depends," I said, squirming. Because if Dad and I aren't going to change back, even though I hate playing the Executive Banana Game, I want to stay here and marry Miss Moon—after all, I certainly can't stay married to Mom and I certainly do love Miss Moon. . . . I wonder if Miss Moon loves me—

"On what?" asked Miss Moon.

But suppose we do change back? Dad doesn't want to be married to Miss Moon, he wants to be married to Mom—hey, wait a minute—

"On what?" repeated Miss Moon, a little more insistently this time.

"Wait a minute, I'm thinking," I told her. This was important: Dad wants to be married to Mom, yes—but more than he wants to be chairman of the board? Mom doesn't think so, but I think so. I hope so. Better be so, because I definitely do not see myself as a child from a broken home. Should I resign from this job and ask for my old one back to save the marriage? But with my luck, it'll turn out we stay the way we are and I'm stuck in New York and—Oh, I dunno, I dunno, I dunno, I dunno, I dunno-o-o!

"On *what!*" said Miss Moon, pink in the face with exasperation. "Time's up, Bill, what does it depend on, tell me—*what?!*" she begged, flinging her hands palm up under my nose.

Okay, Miss Moon, you asked for it!

"On how long I'm going to be stuck in the body of my father and he's going to be stuck in mine."

Miss Moon never missed a beat. In the same straightforward tone she might have used to discuss whose Magic Marker belonged to whom, she said, "This is not your body?"

"No, it's positively not."

"Right," she said calmly, her hand creeping casually toward the intercom box. "Now tell me again, where did you say your body was?"

"At camp in Maine with my father in it"—and here's where I noticed her finger pressing down the intercom button, and realized, too late, that except for the blood-red talons, we seemed to be enacting the very scenario I'd imagined the day I was waiting to be fired.

"Hey, what are you doing that for!" I exclaimed, and here's where she's going to whisper to Betty Lou about the little men in the white coats.

"Okay, okay, I'll go," I moaned, "but if Dad and I

change bodies again while I'm in the cookie jar, will you give him his old job back?"

Tears were now cascading down my cheeks and stinging like fury in my shaving cuts. . . .

"Betty Lou," said Miss Moon, "Mr. Andrews and I would like not to be disturbed for a while, so cancel my ten-thirty meeting and hold all calls, please.

"Come"—she beckoned. "Everything's going to be all right, just come with me."

Obediently, I followed her to an inner-sanctum sitting room I didn't even know existed, where on request, I began with the body exchange in the Port Authority terminal and ended with, "So what you see before you is a twelve-year-old boy"—here's where I started to cry again—"who's very scared and homesick and Mom's mad at me and Dad probably is mad at me, too—well, anyway, now do you see the problem?"

"Yes, I do," she said gravely. "And I think I also see a solution."

"What is it?" I asked. "I'll do anything you say, just tell me what it is."

"A leave of absence, Bill, a good, long leave of absence."

She didn't believe me. I should have known.

"In the cookie jar, you mean."

"No, no." She patted my hand reassuringly. "Nothing like that. Just some time off to calm the nerves and mend the marriage. Maybe you and your wife would like to take a little trip together—"

"That is the last thing in the world we would like," I said, honking furiously into a Kleenex. I was so angry and disappointed with her I could hardly wait to leave. But first, "Where's your bathroom? I want to wash my face."

"Here," she said meekly, leading me to it and snapping on the light.

And there it was! Hanging on the wall just to the right of the sink. Framed and everything.

"Oh!" I marveled, standing practically in the shower to get a better view. "What a great stegosaurus!"

"Yes, isn't it," she agreed. "And how clever of you to know what it was." She cocked her head to one side and admired it fondly. "Most people are totally baffled."

"Listen, if I don't know what it is, who would?" I said, leading her on.

She refused to be led. "Mmn?" She gazed at the stegosaurus, lost in thought.

"After all, I'm the one who painted it."

Oblivious to this, too, she cocked her head on the other side and admired the stegosaurus from a different angle.

"A terrific little boy I once taught did it," she mused. "He didn't think it was any good, but I loved it." She smiled. "I loved him."

I could have melted in a puddle on the floor.

"It was mutual," I said, but I don't think she heard this either.

"His name was Ben . . ." She reached into her memory.

"Andrews," I said.

At last she woke up. "Right," she said, turning slowly to face me. "How did you— Oh!" She recognized me, finally. "Oh, no wonder you looked so familiar, Bill. You're Ben's father, aren't you! Ben Andrews' father! How *is* Ben?"

"I'm fine," I said.

"Yes, I can see that, Bill," she said briskly, "but how is Ben?"

I didn't know what to answer. I couldn't just keep on saying I'm fine, I'm fine, could I? What good would that do, she was never going to believe me anyway.

In silence, I let her steer me to the door.

"Good-bye for now," she said. "And when you see Ben, will you give him a kiss for me?"

I decided to make one last try. "Miss Moon, why won't you believe me?" I pleaded. "You always leveled with me, I always leveled with you, why would I lie to you now?"

There was a long, awkward pause, and then all of a sudden she lit up.

"You know what?" she said. "I think I do believe you. I'm probably out of my mind, and you're probably out of yours, but I really do believe you."

"You do?!" I whispered. "How come?"

"Because," she said, gurgling with laughter, "you haven't changed a bit. Look at you!"

I looked to see where she was looking. At my right leg. Storking on my left leg.

I destorked and grinned at her. "Okay, then, how about my kiss?"

She planted a lovely one right on my cheek. That's where you'd kiss a twelve-year-old boy, isn't it, on the cheek?

Good-bye, Miss Moon. I love you.

July 14th didn't turn out so badly after all.

Eighteen

"There she is," said Annabel, spotting Ellen among the Soonawissavisitors waiting in front of the admin building.

I took off like a bat out of hell.

"Try not to make a complete jackass of yourself," she shouted after me. "She's only your mother!"

As if I needed reminding.

Even so, it wasn't easy. After being separated from your wife for over two weeks, a bear hug, a kiss on the forehead, and a comment on how much you've grown and how great you look is hardly a reunion to gladden the heart of the average man.

"You look great, too . . ." I might as well get used to saying it, "Mom," I managed to squeeze out.

"My sentiments exactly," said Annabel, with a kiss-kiss, a hug-hug, and an anxious "Where's Dad?"

"Dad?" said Ellen, stalling for time.

"Yeah, Dad—the one with the beard and the big blue eyes, remember him?" said Annabel.

Ellen usually responds to Annabel's teasing with some snappy comeback of her own. This time, her response was a deliberately vague "Uh, well . . ."

Annabel raised her eyebrows at me: Trouble in paradise? Ellen saw her and hurriedly continued. "I think he's coming directly from the Coast. I drove up with the Levines." Hm. "Aren't you going to say hello to them, Ben?" she added brightly.

"Sure." As soon as I figure out who they are. "Where are they?" I asked, hoping Ellen would pinpoint them in the group of parents I was pretending to squint at on the admin porch.

"Any closer—"

"—we would have bitten you," said Duck's parents, who were standing right next to us. With half a brain, I could have figured that one out. Not only was Duck standing between them, all three were standing in fifth position. (Aren't genes extraordinary, or do we attribute this one to environmental influence?)

More hellos and hugs, and then Ellen put her foot in it.

"I assume you two guys are still thick as thieves," she said, affectionately rumpling Duck's hair.

Annabel nudged Ellen in the ribs.

"Not exactly," said Duck quietly. Then he turned on his heel and walked off, leaving the rest of us, including his parents, with egg on face and a large conversational void to fill.

"Kids," said Dr. Levine with an uneasy shrug.

"They'll work it out. Won't you," said Mrs. Levine, smiling at me. (Nice woman, Mrs. Levine, a lot like Ellen, no wonder they get along.)

"Hope so," I answered.

"I'm sure," said Ellen.

More silence.

"Where's Dad?" I finally said.

"Yes, where *is* Dad?" echoed Annabel. "They're going to start the exhibition games in a minute, why isn't he here, Mom?"

"Annabel, how would I know," said Ellen irritably. "If he came straight from the Coast, he'd have to fly from Boston to Bangor and rent a car from there."

"No way!" I declared. After what I told him about driving, he wouldn't dare. "That means he's not coming."

"Oh no?" crowed Annabel triumphantly. "Then what is that?" she said, her sharp eyes riveted on the camp entrance.

Turning in was a Buick station wagon, driver in front, passenger in back. Over the rutted road it came, bumping and bouncing and all the while beeping and finally stopping a few feet away.

"What is that is right!" said Ellen in disgust, as the driver deferentially opened the door for a husband she seemed none too pleased to see.

"What *is* that?" I said under my breath after Ape Face and I had greeted each other publicly. "What have you done to my face, that face looks terrible, I almost didn't recognize it! Where's the beard?"

"It'll grow," said Ape complacently. I know where he got that from; it's my automatic rejoinder to his complaint about a too-short haircut.

"Oh well, why should I care, it's not my face," I said.

"Daddy, Daddy, Daddy, what happened to your poor little self!" lamented Annabel, caressing a Band-Aid on his chin. What a disgusting display—if she knew that was her *brother* inside there!. . .

"Hello, Bill," said Ellen, keeping her distance.

With a hesitant "hi," Ape Face approached and kissed her gingerly on the cheek.

"Is that the best you can do?" said Annabel. "What's the matter with you guys!"

"Mind your own business," I told her, although privately I agreed. Ape Face's reticence was understandable, but after being separated from your husband for over two weeks, he merits more than a cool hello. In other words, something was definitely the matter with Ellen.

"Oh!" enthused Ape Face, sighting the Levines.

He bounded over to say hello, I bounded after him, but too late. He was already into "Hi, Dr. Levine, hi, Mrs. Levine!" cordially pumping the doctor's hand and kissing the doctor's wife more heartily than he'd kissed his own mother.

The Levines, glassy-eyed with nonrecognition, tried to cover with the usual nice to see you again's, and I tried to intervene.

"Dad—" I began.

"I get it!" said Ape Face, thinking he knew what was wrong. "You two don't know me without my—"

"Dad, they don't know you at all," I reminded him.

"Well, you do now," he said with a giggle. "Bill Andrews here, great to meet you after all these years!" More hand pumping and cheek kissing, followed by "Where's Duck?"

"Well," said Mrs. Levine, "I think he's—"

"Never mind, I see him, hey Duck!" he yelled, "How are you?"

Duck, undoubtedly torn between wanting to avoid me and greet my nice father who'd sent him batteries, waved tentatively, but stayed put.

"Duck!" yelled Ape again. "C'mere! C'mon over here!"

Duck reluctantly did. "Hello, Mr. Andrews. Thanks loads for the batteries."

"Sure, Duck. Oh, wow, Duck, am I glad to see you! Wow!" rejoiced Ape Face.

"When did you two get so clubby?" said Annabel, arriving on the scene with Ellen.

"At the Port Authority terminal, love at first sight," said Ape Face, on the ball this time. "Like father like son, right, Son?" he asked me. "Right, Duck?"

Duck licked his lips nervously. Ape Face picked up on it immediately. "You two okay?" he asked, his eyes zigzagging back and forth from one of us to the other.

"Bill, I'd leave it alone if I were you," quietly cautioned Ellen.

Ape Face ignored her. "Still best friends and everything?" he asked us.

"Oh, yes," said I.

"No," said Duck coldly. "Ben's best friend is Brian Hitzigger now."

"Brian Hitzigger!" Ape Face roared at me. "Brian *Hitzigger?!*"

"Attila the Hun," Annabel explained to Ellen.

"So I've heard," said Ellen.

"Oh, dear," said Mrs. Levine, commiserating eye-wise with her husband. They, too, had obviously heard of Brian Hitzigger.

Ape Face simply couldn't get over it. "What did you have to do to get *him* on your team?" he said in a tone of blistering contempt.

"Nothing! He was making fun of me in the dining room so I knocked him out cold on the floor—"

"You *did*?!" He was momentarily diverted by this bit of news.

"Yes I did, and he's been crazy about me every since. But that's not my fault, is it? *Is* it?" I asked Duck.

"Maybe not," acknowledged Duck, "but you're also best friends with Baker Biddle, Sandy de Menocal—"

"Never heard of them," said Ape Face.

"Superjocks," said Duck, plunging the dagger in deeper, "with nothing in the noodle. The last of the fetal pigs."

"Not to mention Roland de Berganza, son of the Marquesa de Berganza y Santa Lopez," suggested Annabel snidely. Whose team is she on, I'd like to know.

"He's not a friend, he's a rich wimp!" I said but nobody paid any attention.

"And best, *best* friends with Thor Swensen," said Duck, giving the dagger a final twist.

"The hell I am!" I shouted. "Duck, listen to me. I have one best friend and one only, and that's *you*."

"Oh, yeah? Prove it!" said Duck, blinking back the tears.

Ape Face tried to defuse the issue. "Duck, who's Thor Swensen?"

"Number-One tennis player, your son is number two," said Duck. "Any minute you can see for yourself."

"Now listen up, all you Soonawissafolk," bellowed Wilking through the bullhorn.

"Like right now," said Duck bitterly.

"For the next hour, it's our pleasure to present to you Soonawissakit's finest solo athletes as they demonstrate their prowess in exhibition waterskiin', archery, riflery, rock climbin', wrestlin', tennis—"

"Starring Swensen and Andrews," said Duck.

"—and track," concluded Wilking. "Last but not least"— his voice implying quite the opposite—"there's Ping-Pong for the kids not doin' anythin' else, cuz after all, what's good enough for the Chinese is good enough for us."

Laughter and applause from the parents.

"Excuse me, everybody," I whispered as Wilking started reading out the names of Soonawissakit's finest solo athletes. "I'll be right back"—which I was, in time to hear his pseudogracious concession to Soonawissakit's nonathletes.

"Also durin' this hour's gonna be exhibitions of arts 'n' crafts—which includes loom weavin', metalwork, tie-dyin', and suchlike, plus nature studies pertainin' to various flora and fauna indigenous to the Maine terrain, plus a photography and watercolor exhibit in the dinin' hall for folks whose kids've been fancyin' that kinda activity." God help 'em!

"Now after that's gonna be exhibition team sports of lacrosse, soccer, and baseball; and for the kids not participatin' in any a them, we got a tug-a-war with a rope, and a three-legged race, followed by a picnic lunch on the grass, such as it is—more like pebbles and pine needles, heh-heh-heh—for every-dang-body in the place!

"So go to it, Soonawissafolk, and have yourselves a real nice day."

Applause, applause, applause.

Then, just as the Andrews/Levine contingent was about to disperse, Swensen appeared, sparkling white from teeth to toe, and rarin' to go.

"Ready, partner?" he asked me, taking a few impeccable backhand swipes at an imaginary ball with his graphite racket.

"Golly, Swensen, you're going to think this is ruhlly scuzzy of me, but I've decided to play Ping-Pong with Levine instead."

For probably the first and the last time ever, Duck and Swensen reacted identically. Both their mouths dropped open.

Swensen recovered first. "You're dumping me for Levine?"

"Why not? I dumped Levine for you once. Maybe this'll even up the score," I said, looking first at Ape Face, then at Duck, then back to Swensen. "Don't sweat it, pal, I've already fixed you up with Gorsuch. He's number three, and ruhlly dying to take you on.

"Ready, partner?" I asked Duck as Swensen stalked off in a snit.[*]

"How do you know I want to play?" said Duck. "Maybe you dumped Swensen for nothing."

"Seeing as I dumped you for less, Duck, that's the chance I took."

"He's better, he'll beat you," warned Ape Face. He was testing, testing.

"I'll take that chance, too," I said, passing the test. . . .

And losing the match. Not on purpose, either. In full view of all the Andrews, Levines, and assorted others, he beat me fair and square—he happens to be a better player.

But not a better runner! After Ping-Pong, we paired up for the three-legged race and came in—well, let me describe it this way: When one person is running straight ahead and the other person is running due left because that's the direction his free foot is facing, it's extremely difficult to progress.

We not only didn't come in first, we didn't even come in last; about halfway to the finish line, we fell flat on our faces and just sat there laughing and scratching and hooting and hollering—Duck Levine and the panty-hose queen, joined at the hip forever (metaphorically speaking)—we never came in at all.

---

[*] Somewhat akin to a huff but minus the wheels

At the awards ceremony before lunch, when amidst cheers and huzzahs and humorous catcalls from all the other losers in the camp* Duck and I received the Soonawissabooby Prize, I don't know who was the most delighted—Duck, me, Ape Face . . . or Swensen!

---

* Who seemed like a nice gang—I made a mental note to get to know them better

Nineteen

The picnic lunch (soggy paper plates of lukewarm whole wheat spaghetti with "meat" sauce, gritty lettuce, fruit, cookies, milk) was pretty bad. Not that it mattered. The four of us weren't hungry anyway. And the atmosphere was awful. Annabel and I tried to make cheerful conversation but we kept running into trouble.

"Wasn't that three-legged race the funniest thing you've ever seen in your life, Mom? Dad?" she said.

"Mm-hm, oh, yes," said Mom, making a valiant effort to be jolly. "And I'm sure Duck appreciated your entering it with him, darling." She patted Dad on the shoulder.

"Right you are!" I said. "Making up with Duck is worth a booby prize any old day, don't you think, Ellen?"

"Yes, I think," she said with a slight emphasis on the "I," meaning "that's what *I* think but I'm surprised it's what the future chairman of the board thinks."

"Me, too!" said Annabel. "Besides, Ape Face can

afford a booby prize after what happened last Sunday. Ape, tell them what happened on Sunday."

"I was named Soonawissacamper of the Week," said Dad. "No big deal," he added modestly.

"Nonsense, it means you were the best," said Mom with another shoulder pat for him and a sarcastic crack for me. "Dad must be very proud of you."

"Well I am—very. Aren't you?" I asked her.

"I thought I'd already indicated as much," she said. Thunk. Silence.

A look of alarm shot from Annabel to Dad to me.

I looked down at my plate and carved tic-tac-toe marks on it with my plastic knife until I could see pine needles coming through the bottom.

Annabel made a second attempt. "Say," she said animatedly, "how does everybody like Dad without a beard?"

"It's a little hard to tell right now," said Dad, tactfully referring to the scabs and the Band-Aid, "but I think I liked him better with it."

"It'll grow," I said again. "It's got some stubbly stuff already, see, Annabel?"

Annabel ran her fingers against the grain on my cheek. "Grr," she growled to show approval. In a pinch, she's a real trouper.

"And you, Mom," she asked. "How do *you* like Dad without the beard?"

"About as much as I liked him with it." Mom smiled sweetly at nobody in particular but especially not me.

"Okay!" Annabel blew up. "I've had enough of this—absolutely enough!" She snapped her fork in half. "What's going on here! Mom, Dad, did you two have a fight or something?"

"No. Absolutely no!" I declared.

Mom cleared her throat delicately, meaning "he's a great big liar!"

"Then what's she so mad at?" said Annabel, nodding at Mom.

"That's what I'd like to know," said Dad, glaring at me.

"Well," I sighed, "because of the move, I guess. See, when I got offered the California job, Mom wasn't around to discuss it with, so I said yes, forgetting all about her job in New York—"

"You didn't!" said Dad. "That's appalling!"

"I know, I know," I said, distractedly twirling spaghetti strands around my plate with my finger.

"Bill, stop playing with your food, you're worse than Ben," said Mom crossly. At least she was still talking to me.

I licked my finger and looked pleadingly at her. "But I thought you had . . . we had a different kind of marriage than we do. I thought . . . I thought . . ." I surrendered. "I didn't think, period. I'm really sorry."

"Well," said Mom, relenting somewhat.

"Well, nothing!" said Dad. "It's just the most inconsiderate thing I ever heard in my life!"

"Listen, Mr. Holier Than Thou," said Annabel to Dad, "what are you trying to do—make things worse? If I remember correctly, when that letter arrived, you never gave a thought to Mom's job either—all you were concerned about was having to live in Westwood!"

Dad looked as though he'd been punched in the stomach. "True," he admitted, hanging his head, "I'm afraid that's true."

"Sweetie," Mom reminded Annabel, "he's only a child."

"That makes two of us," I said to Dad.

"No wonder you're upset," said Dad to Mom.

"Oh, I'm not all that upset," she said, back to nice and normal. "Just a little ticked off. And a little worried." She frowned. "What *are* we going to do, Bill?"

"I've been given a leave of absence to think it over, if that's anything," I told her.

"Swell," she said. "But after the leave of absence, what then?"

"I don't know," I said. "I just don't know. Could you and the kids maybe stay in New York, and I could commute back and forth?"

"Commute!" shrieked Annabel. "That's some commute! I don't understand. Don't you two love each other anymore?"

"Yes, we do," said Mom and Dad together.

Annabel scowled at Dad. "Not you, dummy, *you*," she said to me.

"Yes!" I said. "But . . ."

"Could you . . . uh, you could . . . quit," suggested Dad tentatively.

"Not in a million years," said Mom, turning to me for confirmation. "Would you. I know you."

"No, because I'd lose my stock options and severance pay," I said, showing off for Dad. "But I could make them fire me."

"Would you?" Mom looked at me with surprise mixed with what—excitement? hope?—both?

I had an idea. "Ape Face," I said, "if you had to choose between your wife and your job, which would you choose?"

"Oh for heaven's sake, what are you asking him for?" said Annabel. "What would he know about it?"

"More than you think," said Dad. He gave me a decisive nod. "I'd choose my wife."

"That's good to know," I said. "And so would I."

"Oh, Willy!" Mom squeezed my hand.

"Would?" said Annabel. "What do you mean, would?" She's got bat's ears, my sister.

"It's not so simple," I said.

"Oh." Mom withdrew her hand.

"Dad, can I talk to you alone? I've got to talk to you alone!" said Dad.

"Excuse us," I said, and we went for a walk in the woods.

Twenty

Now that we were alone, I didn't know where to begin. We went quite a long way in silence.

He said he wanted to talk, why doesn't he talk! And he'd better have some answers, because my brain is on strike.

"You go first."

He probed a scab on his chin.

"Would you mind leaving my face alone?" Great beginning, Bill, just great. Sounds positively hostile. It was meant to be funny—

"It's not your face anymore, remember? You said so yourself."

—but naturally, he didn't take it that way.

I aimed my foot at a toadstool and kicked it to smithereens.

"I can do anything I want to with this face," he said, glowering down at me. "I might even get it lifted!"

Now that *is* funny. When he gets mad he's really funny.

"What are you laughing at?"

"Nothing, sport." I didn't know he ever got mad. Good

for him. He's human after all.

I reached up to touch him.

"Quit it," he said, ducking out of the way.

I don't know why I did that. He was only trying to be nice.

This kid isn't just mad, this kid is about to self-destruct—do something! I don't know how. Do anything.

"Hey, Ben? Benjie? Listen, we're in this together, we've got to solve it together. I need your help."

His voice was so . . . different, gentle sort of, it took me by surprise. For a second, I couldn't say anything.

Come on, kid, aren't you even going to meet me halfway?

"Yeah, I know, Dad. I'm sorry."

"It's okay."

"You want to sit down? Here's a flat place."

"Why not?" I got partway down.

"Or would you rather keep walking till we come to a rock so I won't get pine tar on your pants?"

"They're your pants now. And it doesn't matter anyway—here is fine, but whatever you want to do."

Why are people always asking me what *I* want to do? I don't know what I want to do, I *never* know what I want to do, I'm sick of it!

"Sit, I guess."

"Fine." I went the rest of the way down.

I think I'm going to jump out of my skin. . . . Better not, who knows whose skin you'll jump into next—

could be Millicent Ewald—uch! or Hitzigger. Oh, sit down and think of something to say, it's your turn and he's waiting. I can't think of anything. I *can't*.

He sighed heavily and looked away.

"I guess it's been rough these last couple of weeks—yes?. . . No?"

He wouldn't look at me and he wouldn't answer, just stared vacantly into the Maine woods. Poor little guy, what in God's name was he thinking now?

I can't stand it when he's nice to me! He's being *so* nice to me . . . I think I'm going to cry.

Ah. So that was it.

"I haven't got much of a shoulder these days, but you're welcome to what there is of it."

I must've been making a terrible face because he asked, "What's the matter now?"

"It stings in the cuts."

I wiped the tears away with my hand. "Where? Which one?"

"This one," he said, pointing—just like when he was three.

He kissed it. "Better?" he wanted to know, just like when I was little.

"Yes," he whispered. "Are you crying, too? You look as though you're crying, too."

"What do you want from me?" he said, scrambling to his feet. "I'm only a little kid."

I laughed, and got to my feet, too.

The tension was gone, now, but not the sadness.

"Yeah, well, I wish you weren't," he said ruefully. "I want to be the little kid and you be the grown-up. I'm not ready. It's too hard," he said, storking on my pants—*his* pants! "Much too hard."

"Oh, no it's not," he said, trying to cheer me up. "You've already missed the hard part. What's ahead is all downhill sledding. I'm the one you ought to feel sorry for. I've got to live through all that rotten stuff all over again.

"I'd much rather be you," "I'd much rather be you," we both said at once, and for the second time in one week, I crashed to the ground. Storking is simply not one of my talents.

"Jeeze Louise, Ape Face, look what you made me do to my pants!" I said, examining a colossal triangular rip in the knee. I must have been in shock. I mean, after enduring two hideous weeks of imprisonment in your son's body, not to mention his world, when you finally get your own body back, you don't complain about pants!

Ape Face had a firmer grip on reality. "Better yours than mine," he said with a wild and wicked guffaw. "Boy, am I glad that's over!"

Then he fell into my outstretched arms and snuggled there cosily while we

1) Exchanged factual information about our experiences in L.A. and Soonawissakit—not in any great detail, just hitting the highlights—at the end of which, Ape said, "Say, Dad, you

know that composition they always make us write in the fall—'How I Spent My Summer Vacation'? Well?" He wiggled his eyebrows up and down rapidly like Groucho Marx. "What do you think?"

What I thought I won't disclose now. What I said was "I wouldn't, if I were you."

"Ha-ha-ha, but you're not!" he said gleefully. I'm telling you, once this kid gets started, there's no stopping him—he was full of beans.

He also knows when enough is enough. "Because of the little men, you mean?" he asked, sobering up.

"Partly," I told him. "Mostly, I'd just rather you didn't. But there's always the rest of the summer. . . ."

A fleeting cloud crossed his face. "I can hardly wait," he said. "Is this place as bad as it seems?"

"The pits."

"It must have changed since your day, huh, Dad?"

"Not one iota."

"*No?!* Then how come you loved it so much?"

"I didn't. But over the years, I guess I managed to block out the worst of it, so when you wanted to go—"

"But only because I thought it would make you happy!"

"And guess why I wanted to go?"

"To make Grandpa happy?"

I nodded. "And if you send any kid of yours here, I'll break every bone in your body!"

"Poor Duck," said Ape,

which led to

2) A discussion on jocks vs. nonjocks, in which we agreed that being a Soonawissacamper of the Week, i.e. a fabulous superjock, was maybe sixty percent motivation and will, and only forty percent native athletic ability.

"You probably could have done it yourself, Dad," observed Ape.

"What do you mean? I did do it myself!" I said, briefly succumbing to a residual attack of pride.

"In my body," he reminded me.

"With my motivation and will," I reminded him. "If you'd been here, would you have been Soonawissacamper of the Week? No." A sudden, searing insight: "Because aside from motivation and will, it also requires ruthless aggression, and you're too nice."

which led to

3) My admitting that his extraordinary niceness had always awed me to the point where I didn't know how to communicate with him, resulting in all the vapid "how was school?" conversations, including the quintessential feeding-the-fingertip-to-the-guinea-pig incident, for which I humbly begged his forgiveness. He then admitted to me that the guinea pig incident had never actually happened, he'd invented it for Duck in a moment of extreme self-pity, for which he humbly begged *my* forgiveness. I was only too happy to give it.

More important was his admission that what I'd taken to be extraordinary niceness was nothing but Yellow-Jell-O cowardice because he was scared of making people mad at him, in fact he was scared of quite a few things—

"And scared to death of me, I gather."

"I used to be," he said, "but not anymore."

"Well, well, well! And why not?"

"Because it turns out we're so much alike."

"I consider that a compliment," I told him.

"To me or to you?" he said with an impish grin. Cocky kid! I rubbed his face in pine needles till he yelled uncle.

"Ape Face," I said when we'd stopped horsing around, "I'm afraid of things, too. Everybody is."

"Like not having a job?" he asked.

"Yes, just like."

"But you know," he said, "aside from the problem of Mom, from what I've seen of your job, I'm not sure it doesn't take more guts to keep it than to quit."

which led to

4) An indignant monologue from Ape Face on the subject of executive game players like Tony Crane and Ray Ewald; the loneliness of men like Ty Donovan who couldn't afford to trust anybody but their wives—if you didn't have a wife, you were really up the creek (it was phenomenal how much he'd picked up in only a couple of weeks!); and then some juicy philosophizing about how to survive in a business where the thing that counts is not what you are but what people think you are—as evidenced by Miss Moon's Killer Cream Puff coup which worked vs. Ty's indie prod pretense which didn't—

leading finally to

5) Ape's Bottom Line: What kind of banana was I anyway?

194

This was very important for him to know, he said.

I considered myself only a second banana, I told him. Would this be satisfactory?

Quite, he assured me. Actually, it was the only kind he liked.

So, with all that settled, we returned to camp, where we received a somewhat reserved greeting from Ellen and an overly effusive one from Annabel, who had the sleaze bag in tow.

"Daddy! I'd like you to meet my good friend and co-worker, Terry Mallison."

"Sir," said Mallison politely.

Ape Face, being the soul of generosity, was overjoyed to learn that Annabel had found a friend to call her own in this godforsaken place (he had Duck, after all). "Any friend of Annabel's," he said pleasantly.

Annabel, still smarting from the tirade delivered by her little brat brother earlier in the week, misinterpreted this altogether, and countered with an ominous threat. "One more word out of you, Ape!. . ."

"What did I do?" whispered poor bewildered Ape.

"Later," I muttered, "I'll explain later."

"Well," said Ellen to Ape and me, "you two were gone long enough—did you solve the problem?"

Mallison, realizing he was an interloper, slipped away, leaving just the four of us.

"Which one?" said Ape, cheery as a bird dog. "We solved tons of them." Light dawned. "Oh, you mean did we solve

The Problem. Dad!" he turned to me in a panic.

"Don't worry, sport, it's not your problem anymore," I said.

"But it is yours, Willy—ours," said Ellen wistfully. "Didn't you come up with anything in all that time?" She looked at the rip in my pants. "Or were you just fooling around."

I sat down beside her on the grass; Ape and Annabel sat, too.

"Now, here's what," I said, putting my arm around her. "One: you are going to keep your job. Two: I am going to accept that leave of absence. Three: we—meaning just us," I said to Ellen, "are going to fly to L.A. tomorrow to tie up a few loose business ends, and after that comes Number Four. . . ." I kissed her (it's been a long time).

"Which is?" prompted Ellen, kissing me back.

"Malibu or Pebble Beach or somewhere for a nice, long honeymoo—"

"Dad!" said Annabel, gesticulating madly at Ape Face behind his back. "Certain people are allergic to that word, ahem, ahem."

Ape Face, he's no dope, turned around and caught her at it.

"Who me? What's wrong with a honeymoon?" he asked.

"Nothing!" said Ellen.

"I think it's a great idea," said Ape.

"You do? Oh. Well, fine then," said Annabel, understandably nonplussed. "You didn't think it was so great on Wednesday."

"I've had a complete change of mind," he said serenely.

I couldn't have put it nicelier myself.

Twenty-One

Maybe it was just because I was feeling so good about Dad and me, or maybe because I was expecting so much worse, or maybe a combination of the two, but camp turned out to be not so terrible after all.

In fact, between the jocks continuing to like me (although I wasn't quite the athlete Dad had been, owing to lack of motivation and will, I suppose) because I'd once made Soonawissacamper of the Week, and the nonjocks liking me (which they apparently hadn't before) because I'd stuck by Duck on Soonawissavisitors Day, I was getting along just fine with everybody except Swensen, Hitzigger, and Splasher Wilking—them I'm *never* going to like. Duck was getting along fine with everybody, too; not that peer approval is all that important to him anyway— he's perfectly contented with one good friend and a Sony in good, working condition.

In *fact*—this you're going to find hard to believe— since Duck's parents were pretty tied up in New York and mine were still in California, they gladly gave us permission to sign on for the Soonawissakit second session, and we ended up spending a total of eight weeks in the place. (To be accurate, eight for Duck, only six for me.)

A few days before camp was over, I got a letter from Dad.

Dear Ape Face,

I know Mom has written you and I'm sorry I haven't, but I've been extremely busy with some writing of my own—a screenplay, finished last week (untitled as yet), which Ty Donovan considers a hot property and is going to produce in association with Galaxy. Everybody is thrilled and loves it, especially your wonderful Miss Moon.

And what is it about? You may well ask! It's the story of a twelve-year-old boy and his father who spend two weeks in each other's bodies, etc., etc.—you know how it all comes out. (You also know now why I didn't want you to write your "How I Spent My Summer Vacation" composition on this subject. Hope you understand and forgive—after all, it's your story too, but as a full-time writer, which is what I've decided to be, with Mom's blessing, I figured my need for material superseded yours!)

Incidentally, Ty is floored by what he calls my "uncanny ability to crawl into the mind of a kid," and wonders how I managed to do it. Mom, though she's crazy about the screenplay, seems to take this aspect of it for granted; she says I might be amused by a composition Annabel wrote years ago called "Freaky Friday"—she'll dig it out for me when we get home.

Tell Duck more batteries are on the way, and if you could come up with a good title for me, it would be tremendously appreciated. I can't seem to think of anything.

I love you,
Dad.

Twenty-Two

This morning I got a Mailgram saying

HOW ABOUT SUMMER SWITCH?
I LOVE YOU, TOO. APE FACE.

THE END   THE END